SAGA OF BRUTES

Ana Paula Maia

SAGA OF BRUTES

Translated from Brazilian Portuguese
by Alexandra Joy Forman

DALKEY ARCHIVE PRESS

Originally published in Portuguese as *Entre rinhas de cachorros e porcos abatidos* by Editora Record in 2009 and *Carvão animal* by Editora Record in 2011.

First edition, 2016

Library of Congress Cataloging-in-Publication Data
Names: Maia, Ana Paula, author. | Forman, Alexandra Joy, translator.
Title: Saga of brutes / by Ana Paula Maia ; translated from Brazilian Portuguese by Alexandra Joy Forman.
Description: First edition. | Victoria, TX : Dalkey Archive Press, 2016. | Original collection of novellas published as two volumes in Portuguese: *Entre rinhas de cachorros e porcos abatidos* & *Carvão animal.*
Identifiers: LCCN 2016031166 | ISBN 9781628971460 (pbk. : alk. paper)
Subjects: LCSH: Maia, Ana Paula--Translations into English.
Classification: LCC PQ9698.423.A36 A2 2016 | DDC 869.3/5--dc23
LC record available at https://lccn.loc.gov/2016031166

MINISTÉRIO DA CULTURA
Fundação BIBLIOTECA NACIONAL

Partially funded by a grant by the Illinois Arts Council, a state agency.

Obra publicada com o apoio do Ministério da Cultura do Brasil / Fundação Biblioteca Nacional.

Work published with the support of Brazil's Ministry of Culture / National Library Foundation.

www.dalkeyarchive.com
Victoria, TX / McLean, IL / Dublin

Dalkey Archive Press publications are, in part, made possible through the support of the University of Houston-Victoria and its programs in creative writing, publishing, and translation.

Printed on permanent/durable acid-free paper

Contents

BOOK 1. Between Dogfights and Hog Slaughter

And the glory of character is in affronting the horrors of depravity, to draw thence new nobilities of power: as Art lives and thrills in new use and combining of contrasts, and mining into the dark evermore for blacker pits of night.
—Ralph Waldo Emerson

No man should be allowed to be the president who does not understand hogs, or hasn't been around a manure pile.
—Harry Truman, 1945

CHAPTER 1
"You Mustn't Mess with Pigs that Don't Belong to You"

While waiting on pigs, Edgar Wilson takes eight long breaths. It's a hot and humid Friday, but he appears unfocused and unbothered as if he'll patiently wait as long as it takes. Despite these external appearances, he's anxious. It's the second delayed delivery in four days, and he'll have to report it to his boss.

His plans were to get off early in the afternoon and head over to Cristóvão's bar to bet his money on Chacal—the devil-possessed canine that ripped Gepetto's head clear off, and he's twice his size—and then to meet Rosemery, his fiancée. No surprise there, every Friday's the same, and Edgar Wilson doesn't mind the routine. But, forgotten and ignored, at the back of a stinking deli, in a hot and humid suburb, a delayed pig delivery's especially irksome, and nothing's so great as the anticipation to see those pigs hanging from hooks in the freezer.

Edgar Wilson's counting on the new moon to put a spark under Chacal's paws. He plans to triple his bet, and then pop the question. Rosemery insists on a new refrigerator to definitively seal their romance, and these winnings could buy it. Rosemery's commitment has been a bit problematic of late. She's been overnighting at the house of a lady she cleans for, allegedly to start work at dawn on Tuesday and Thursday mornings. It's characteristic of his personality not to think too hard on these matters. He believes Divine Providence bears our heaviest burdens, and in Divine Providence he puts all his faith. As Father Guilhermino

Anchieta used to say, "Why worry yourself if it doesn't make you any taller or put hair on your chest?" Between dogfights and slaughtered hogs, Edgar Wilson doesn't like to complain about life.

Hearing the faraway roar of a motor, he stamps his cigarette out on a mess of ants constellating where he last spit. His phlegm is reddish, and he briefly ponders infection. He checks his watch, pulls on some rubber boots, and stands. As he waits for the approaching pickup, he picks up the phone behind the counter. He calls his assistant Gerson, who's home with a renal crisis.

"Didn't you give a kidney to your sister?"

"Last year."

"Right. Delivery's late, again."

"Second time this week."

"I'll have to tell the boss."

"Sorry, Edgar, the kidney has me . . ."

"I know."

"I can send Pedro."

"Can he debone?"

"Wait a minute."

Gerson shifts in the sofa to get comfortable, he's in pain and has the cold sweats, he then yells: "Pedro, can you debone?"

In time, Pedro appears wearing only a red towel, a wooden spatula in hand.

"Baking?" asks Gerson.

"A cake."

"You bought flour?"

"No. I took what was in the blue container."

"Did you forget what I told you, Pedro . . .?"

"What?"

". . . about the wheat flour in the blue container."

Pedro raises the wooden spatula and licks the dripping batter. He chews and inhales. Delicious batter. Pedro is pleased.

Swallowing: "What was it?" he asks.

"Worms. I told you to throw it out."

Pedro scratches his head and replies, "I sifted out the worms."

Gerson doesn't react.

"Sifted all of it. Truth."

Gerson turns his attention back to the TV. Pedro stands there with the wooden spatula, and they laugh along with the canned laughter of the cooking show. Pedro notices his brother's still holding the phone.

"Gerson, didn't you call me?" he asks, pointing to the phone.

"Oh . . . know how to debone?"

Pedro thinks.

"Don't know."

"Edgar wants to know."

"Do you mean separating the innards, the liver, the . . ."

"The meat from the bone . . . these things."

Pedro thinks some more, without a word goes to the kitchen. And returns.

"Do you remember Tinho, Matilda's dog?"

Gerson nods, though he's confused. The towel slips from Pedro's waist.

"Those are my underpants," says Gerson. Pedro says nothing, heads back to the kitchen.

"Edgar, remember when Matilda's dog, Tinho, was gutted?"

"Yes."

"Pedro did it."

"Then tell him they've been delivered. And what about the good kidney, the one that's with your sister?"

"I think it's okay."

"Have you thought about asking for it back? I mean you didn't need it when you gave it to her, but now that's different."

"Yes. She's got cancer."

"She won't need it for very long."

"No, don't think so. Listen up. Did I leave the Chuck Norris at your house?"

"*Missing in Action?*"

"*Braddock: Missing in Action III.*"

"I've only got *Missing in Action II*. Not *III*, no."

"Shit, I lost it. That leaves a major hole in my collection."

Silence.

"Are you going to let your sister's cancer eat your healthy kidney?"

"Her hair's falling out."

"Right . . . and the radiation will probably kill your kidney."

"Think so?"

"I think your kidney's a has-been."

***

Pedro crouches at the back of the store stroking the pig that waits to be slaughtered while Edgar Wilson, leaning on the pickup outside, resolves some issues.

Edgar to the driver: "Now I'll say it for the tenth time—I was expecting two pigs."

"But this one's worth two."

"No way, man. I need two pigs. That was the deal. My boss won't accept it."

"Lost one on the road. Potholes."

"Lost one? Who loses a pig. Don't dick me around. I want two pigs."

"I brought you a very big pig. Help yourself."

The pickup skids out of the yard, blowing dust in Edgar Wilson's eyes.

***

"Pedro, stop kissing the pig and pick up the knife over there," says a sullen Edgar Wilson, thinking he's just been had. If he doesn't find a solution, it'll come out of his own pocket. On his salary, there won't be much left at the end of the month.

Pedro points to some intestines in a bucket on the table.

"When I cut Tinho open, there was less stuff."

"That's a hefty hog. Not a skinny dog like Tinho, all wind inside," mutters Edgar, grabbing hooks from the table.

"There was a frog."

Edgar faces Pedro, pensive.

"Yes, sir. A frog. And it was alive too," says Pedro, excitedly.

"What planet are you from?"

Edgar Wilson picks up an ax from the floor.

Pedro brings him the knife and stands next to him.

"The damn dog had a live frog in its stomach. No shit!"

"What did you do with the frog?"

"Named her Gilda. Put her in a cage."

Edgar directs Pedro to put the knife on the floor and hold the hog steady. Pedro tries, but the pig slips from his hands.

"Don't let it escape," yells Edgar.

"The knife spooked it," Pedro snaps back, running after the hog.

The hog throws its weight around despairingly, bangs into the table, overturning a bucket of innards. One of the hooks left behind by Edgar falls on the animal, sticks its pink flesh, burrows into a rib. The beast crashes through some barbed wire, cutting itself up as it squeezes through but the hook catches the wire, and it squeals increasingly in pain and anguish as it forces its way to the other side. Pedro carefully attempts to cut the hog loose but when it feels Pedro's breath on its nape, it freaks out even more and frees itself. The lodged hook pulls back its flesh exposing a succulent rib. Edgar Wilson and Pedro jump the fence into the neighbor's yard. The pig runs toward the chicken coop sending hens cackling and one launches into Edgar Wilson. He yelps, arms aflutter; he jumps back over the fence, ripping his pants. Pedro finally catches the hog and brings it back, squealing. He laughs his ass off at Edgar Wilson.

"What the hell, Edgar . . . you chicken?"

"Shut up and bring the damned swine over here!" Edgar

Wilson, collecting himself.

"Never seen anything so desperate," says Pedro.

"I have."

Edgar Wilson has a rare, irrational, disproportionately morbid, and persistent aversion to chickens. He's ashamed of it and keeps it a secret.

Pedro holds the sow firmly, while Edgar gets the ax.

"Don't let it loose again," mutters Edgar. He lights a cigarette. Raises the ax, stops midair. A wrinkle of doubt spans his forehead. He lowers his arm and purses his lips in doubt: "Why'd you keep the frog?"

"Gilda's a survivor. A small creature with a big will for life. She's an example of strength," responds Pedro, thoughtfully.

Satisfied, Edgar Wilson raises the ax and drops it on the pig's head, which rolls to one side as it emits a final, horrible grunt and sneezes blood, a straight shot into Pedro's left eye. He jumps back.

"You know your brother really misses that Braddock film."

Pedro sees red and goes to wash his eye out at the sink. "Miserable pig," he complains. Still bending over the sink, he asks: "*Missing in Action III?*"

Edgar Wilson stands by the window and looks out at the sky. He's thinking that if the new moon isn't sufficiently pretty, Chacal may not have a chance against the other dog tonight.

"You'd better get it back from your friend," says Edgar.

"He moved," says Pedro walking away from the sink, face cleaned, vision repaired.

"Bring the knife," says Edgar Wilson drying sweat from his face and dragging on his smoke, before bending over the animal.

"Don't know when he'll be back. He doesn't live here anymore. I'd practically have to go across town."

"Figure it out. He wants that video. It matters to him."

With some effort, he mechanically perforates the pig's heart, which spurts blood under pressure of the blade. The phone rings.

Edgar thinks how this Friday afternoon has become messy. He wipes his hands on his already soiled apron and goes to get the phone.

"It's still alive!"

"It'll bleed out at most five minutes," says Edgar Wilson. "Then we'll open it up."

"What do I do?"

"Pick up that offal."

***

"Hello?"

"Edgar, I think you're right."

"Gerson?"

"I need my kidney back in its place."

"You really think so?"

"Absolutely."

"I agree."

Silence.

"So we both agree."

"Yup." Edgar Wilson shoos a fly from his face.

"Is everything okay?"

"I need to get back."

He hangs up the phone and takes a sip of coffee with a piece of day-old bread. He chews for a few seconds and goes back to the knackery—that's what he calls the improvised slaughterhouse at the back of the deli. On the ground, animal blood; in the air, an iron odor. Against the wall, Pedro, moaning, getting it off on an animal he calls Rosemery. While he takes the hog doggy-style, at each thrust, a yellowish liquid runs from its torn breast.

"Rosemery," murmurs Edgar Wilson.

Pedro slows his moves on the hog and, finishing, pulls up his pants.

"Rosemery?!" Edgar Wilson insists.

Pedro, head down, has no words. Edgar coldly orders Pedro to get a bottle of alcohol from behind the bar. He obeys.

Silently, he pours alcohol over the animal and then torches it. A bonfire separates Edgar Wilson from Pedro, while the pig singes quickly. Edgar looks at the incandescent swine with a glint in his eye. Hot from the fire, he turns his gaze on Pedro.

"I don't think you should be going around putting your business in pigs that don't belong to you."

Pedro, somewhat timorously looks to Edgar Wilson and stutters:

"Your boss doesn't need to know."

Edgar gets a pail of water and puts out the fire on the already crisp animal. The smell is unbearable. Pedro fearfully holds his ground on the other side of the rising, gray stinging smoke. With a cleaver, Edgar Wilson begins to scrape the pork hide. He stops and points the blade at Pedro.

"Just scrape."

Pedro takes the blade from Edgar's hands and bends over the pig. As he scrapes the carbonized hide, a sob escapes his throat.

Edgar Wilson walks into the deli and calls Gerson.

"Is that Braddock video really so important?"

"Yes, but I can get another. Of course there's the sentimental value, but what can we do?"

"That's all I wanted to know."

Edgar Wilson returns to the knackery, and to Pedro, silently scraping pork hide. He picks a machete up off the floor and approaches the boy. Lights a cigarette, takes a long drag, and is reinvigorated. While he looks at Pedro, he thinks of Rosemery. He raises the machete and busts the man's head, which spins to the right. Pedro falls over. He convulses. Maybe she likes fruit magnets. He could easily get her some. But he can't remember her favorite fruits. This upsets him. Pedro continues to jerk.

"What's her favorite fruit?"

Edgar bends over Pedro and asks again. Pedro holds his cut

left ear, and looks piously at Edgar, who coldly awaits a response.

His insistent gaze provokes a whispered reply.

"Wild strawberries."

"What devil of a fruit is that? Never heard of it."

"It's something her boss likes."

Pedro holds his ear and trembles. He notices a hole in his head that wasn't there before. He touches humid mass and it's as if he were touching his thoughts.

"What's her second favorite fruit?"

"Peaches," he responds, sobbing.

Edgar murmurs with him, "Peaches." He'll need to write it down before he forgets. He repeats while he walks to the deli counter. He takes note and thinks he never bothered to ask Rosemery what her favorite fruits are. He thinks of wild strawberries and sees strawberries with thorns. At least that's how he imagines them. Strawberries that pierce the lips. He returns to the knackery and Pedro is dragging himself across the floor, moaning, soiling himself in warm pig's blood. Edgar approaches.

"You shouldn't mess with pigs that don't belong to you."

Pedro closes his eyes when he perceives a second blow coming, which smashes his face, deforming it. This reminds Edgar Wilson of what will become of Gerson's kidney if he doesn't do something about it soon. It's especially worrisome.

Edgar Wilson opens the hog from snout to tail and removes its organs and tripe. It's marvelous to look at these innards. A bellyful; worth a pretty penny. And he inwardly complains of the value of a man's labor. The belly of that hog is worth practically his entire salary; but then he feels better, because life is good.

Curious, as only he is, Edgar Wilson tears Pedro in half, removes his organs and admires their weight. Pedro's worth as much as any pig, and his tripe, lungs and maw would offset the loss of another pig. A guy who deceives by appearance. One would never suspect Pedro of having an affair with Rosemery, much less of carrying a fortune in tripe within his belly. Edgar

Wilson is pleased he underestimated Pedro. He'll grind his mortal remains in the meat grinder with the hog's bones and sell them for kibble.

After work, he has two beers at Cristóvão's bar and wins three times what he bet on Chacal. The son-of-a-gun was possessed by the devil. In the sky, a new moon shines and Divine Providence once again relieves him of his too heavy burden. Overcome by so many feelings, he perceives he's very lucky because his salary wasn't docked, and he proposed to Rosemery. Tasting the peaches he brought her and with tears in her eyes she said yes when Edgar promised her a new refrigerator with fruit magnets, the bitch.

CHAPTER 2
"With Tears in their Eyes Even Dogs Eat their Owners"

"Another smoke?"

"No."

Edgar Wilson and Gerson have stopped at a bakery in front of Marinéia's building. Marinéia is Gerson's sister who has guardianship over his healthy kidney. He downs another shot, while Edgar Wilson lights another cigarette.

"So as I was saying . . . when he saw the dogs tearing away with his father's dismembered body parts . . . he went mad," recounts Edgar Wilson.

"I'd go nuts too. I'd unload a magnum on the mutts."

"And that's just what he did. One managed to escape, the other died."

Gerson throws back another shot.

"Wasn't the old goat deaf?" asks Gerson.

"As a doorknob. He went out for a walk with the dog for company, as always, and he forgot to put in his hearing aid. When he crossed the tracks, he didn't hear the whistle," continues Edgar Wilson.

"Why didn't he use the pedestrian overpass?"

"Because of the bums who assault people up there."

"Poor devil."

They're silent for a minute with personal regrets.

"Can't even trust a dog . . . man's best friend," says a solemn Gerson.

"These are difficult times. Even the dogs eat their owners in broad daylight," says Edgar Wilson, taking another drag. "I've heard of this before, it's common. A dog tradition, or instinct, or whatever. They'd rather eat their owners than let vultures get them. Remember those folks on the back street behind Mr. Alípio's place?"

"Of course!"

"They say Fofinho ate all five."

"Fofinho?! He was a fucking poodle!"

"He ate them one by one, while they cried, and later he vomited there, behind Donãna's house. Fofinho ate and purged everyone under a mango tree, son of a bitch."

Silence.

"That must be why those mangoes rotted," says Gerson, tilting back the last drop. "Don't want any damned mutt eating me. If I'm going to be eaten, it should be a tiger, a lion . . . not a gay, pink poodle named Fofinho."

Gerson checks the time on his wristwatch. He asks Edgar to wait just a few more minutes.

"It's absurd your sister won't receive you at home. And it's thanks to you she can still snub you like this. It could make you bitter."

"She's ashamed of the family. Calls us ugly and ignorant. She's a whore . . . only hangs with fancy people. She gave up the family a long time ago," says Gerson.

"She may have, but she didn't disown your kidney," murmurs Edgar, putting out his smoke.

"Must be a fat-ass of gold, this place is cool."

***

The two cross the street and enter the three-story building. The lobby is abandoned. They walk right through and take the stairs.

"I'm expecting a large shipment in today," comments Edgar

Wilson.

"If they're Dona Maria das Vacas's hogs, we'll have double the work."

"I don't know what that old lady gives her hogs . . . they've got endless tripe."

Edgar Wilson reaches the third floor completely out of breath, and Gerson feels pain in his kidney. They pause in front of Apartment 302 and ring the bell.

"Have you heard from Pedro? He disappeared days ago," says Gerson.

"No idea."

They ring the bell again and hear movement inside the apartment.

"Is it true that you and Rosemery are getting married?"

"I popped the question and she said yes."

Gerson gives his friend a big hug, and wishes him happiness.

"A man needs his own family," he says emotionally.

Marinéia unlocks the door and receives them in a red robe with pink trim. She's rather surprised. She doesn't know what to say and searches for the right words. She trips over the formal greetings, forgets the open, welcome smile, and what comes out is "sonofabitch doorman."

"Been a long time, Neínha," says Gerson.

While Marinéia babbles other incomprehensible things, the two invade her small studio. In a few short glances, they familiarize themselves with the place.

"Marinéia, I've come to ask for something back."

"But . . . when did I borrow something from you, Gerson?"

Edgar Wilson sweeps the place with his eyes. He likes a souvenir, a globe with a tiny blue house with yellow doors and windows. When shaken, it fills with snow. He's really enchanted by it.

"Marinéia, how can you say that? I loaned you something more or less a year ago, don't you remember?"

"Gerson, stop mucking about and out with it."

A wide-eyed and startled Chihuahua enters the miniscule living room and brushes against Marinéia's feet until she swoops it up in her arms. Marinéia returns her attention to her brother who's astounded by the videos on the table.

"It's my Braddock film."

"Oh, so that's what you've come to get?" asks Marinéia.

"How did it end up here, Neínha?"

"Pedro asked me to buy it, said he needed money, and I bought it so he'd leave me in peace."

"He did?" perplexed. "And what did you pay for it?"

"I gave him five reais. Look Gerson, you can take the film, I'm not going to watch it anyway."

"Five reais? I paid ten."

Silence.

"Well, if that's all, there's the video."

"That's not what I came to get, but I'll take it with me, for sure."

"Gerson, what the fuck do you want from me?" she says, impatiently.

Gerson finishes looking at the contents of the box and sees that his video is intact.

He sighs relieved.

"I want my kidney back," he mutters.

"Uh? I didn't hear you," says Marinéia, timorously.

"I want my kidney, which you have. I want it back. And I want to use the bathroom."

Marinéia laughs, nervously.

"What do you mean you want your kidney back? Are you crazy, Gerson?"

"I need it." He looks around for the bathroom. "The one I kept isn't doing so well, isn't that right, Edgar? Is the bathroom in there?" He points and heads in the direction of a partially opened door.

Edgar Wilson walks toward the front door and turns the key.

Gerson locks himself in the bathroom leaving the two of them alone in the living room. Edgar seems to want to break the ice. Marinéia holds onto her dog and can't move. She inhales deeply and a desperate sob rises in her throat, keeps her frozen in place. The minutes Gerson is in the bathroom pass densely and quietly until finally broken by the muffled sound of the flush. He's zipping his fly as he leaves the bathroom. Anxiously squeezing the Chihuahua until its eyes seem to pop more, in the middle of the living room, she says:

"You've always been a prankster, right?"

"Néinha, I think you're all mixed up," says Gerson, with restraint. He glances again at the videos and, after a brief pause, continues, "That's what happens when you stay away from home so long."

Confused, she looks at Gerson.

"I was never a prankster."

Edgar Wilson grabs Marinéia and covers her mouth with his hand. She protests and drops the Chihuahua onto the floor; it emits a sharp bark and makes a quick escape under the table. Gerson takes some tape from his backpack and rapidly gags his sister. She doesn't stop squirming, the phone rings, she struggles more brutally. The dog pees, it's trembling so with fear. A punch to the jaw quiets Marinéia down. They lay her on the floor. Gerson tears the phone cord from the wall. Huge stillness invades the small apartment. They approach the bookcase with CDs. Most, they've never heard.

"But Neínha's a beast," says Gerson.

"Look here! It's Sérgio Reis."

They put on the CD and hum along to *Sertaneja* country music while they carry Marinéia to the tub. In the bathroom, there are used condoms on the floor.

"Your sister's a real pig, huh, Gerson?" They throw Marinéia in the bathtub and undress her.

"Here, Edgar, the scar. All we have to do is cut above it."

"Best to cut a little further away to avoid scratching the

organ," adds Edgar.

Gerson opens his backpack and can't find the knife.

"But how'd you forget that?"

"I was in a rush."

Gerson goes into the kitchen and comes back with some things that might help: a can opener, a vegetable slicer, a spoon, and a serrated knife.

"Would you rather I use the can opener or this spoon?"

"Whatever, Edgar."

"Christ! You can't open a person with a spoon, Gerson."

"Oh, no? I bet Braddock could do it," he spits back.

"So why don't you call him?"

Gerson decides to go down to the lobby and ask for help; maybe the doorman has returned by now.

"If I have a pocketknife, son?"

"That's it, yes, sir."

***

Gerson kneels next to Edgar, who examines Marinéia.

"If I'm sincere, you won't be mad will you?"

"Imagine, Edgar."

"I wouldn't have sex with your sister if she paid me."

Gerson looks at his sister.

"At home, everyone's really ugly. And the girls all look like whores."

Edgar Wilson sees what's in Gerson's hands.

"I think this'll work," says Gerson holding up the pocketknife.

"So tiny? And with the Flamengo team logo? Have you taken a good look at your fucking sister? That little blade has no chance against her fat ass."

"But it's all I could find."

"Gerson, fuck, I'm a Vasco fan."

Gerson lowers his head. Edgar's familiar with his friend's drama and knows he must do something, anything, now.

"I need to draw a line around it. See if you can find a marker."

"What for, Edgar? You open pigs every day and don't need any fancy circles drawn on the hogs to cut."

"Gerson, shut your mouth! If I'm asking for something to draw with, you've just got to get it, and keep your mouth shut."

Gerson gets up and crosses the living room, complaining, kicks the Chihuahua, and returns with red lipstick that he hands to Edgar Wilson. He goes to the kitchen and gets two beers. Again he kicks the Chihuahua; it pisses all over the studio.

"I got us some beers."

Edgar takes a gulp and bends over the bathtub. Marinéia wakes, but it's nothing that a well-placed fist can't resolve. He draws a circle around the scar. Then he puts the lipstick in his pocket. He grabs the pocketknife and begins to cut through the fatty, stretch-marked flesh with some force.

"I think that's the kidney, isn't it?"

"You're the specialist here, Edgar."

"Although she looks a lot like a sow, your sister . . ."

"I think that's the liver," interrupts Gerson.

"Do you really? Then, if this is the liver, the kidney must be . . . it's this one," says Edgar Wilson, apparently with some emotion, "It's dark red. That's it!"

Edgar Wilson pokes inside the open cavity with his fingers. He cuts a little more to one side, but the small Flamengo pocketknife doesn't cooperate, and slips vertiginously from one side to the other. Gerson throws some talcum into the cavity to help the precarious instrument handle better. Edgar sneezes uncontrollably; he's allergic to talcum. And with every attempt to cut followed by a sneeze, he finds himself in unexplored places. Slashing Marinéia was never part of his plan, but it's difficult to maneuver the pocketknife precisely and make incisions like a surgeon. He severs the long, thin tube attaching the kidney, and sneezes, and the ungoverned blade glides through the abdominal aorta, rupturing it.

"Damn!"

"What happened?"

"I think I cut something I shouldn't," responds Edgar.

Gerson takes a look and says:

"She's bleeding a lot."

For the first time, Edgar Wilson looks confused.

"I don't get this."

"How many kidneys does she have?"

"I think she's only got the one."

"So what's this?"

"I don't know . . . take this one from beneath the scar. It's the surer bet," says Gerson, pumped now.

"I think we should take these two. Just to be safe," concludes Edgar, carefully removing the organs with the help of a spoon.

"You know something . . . I didn't want to tell you this, but since we're friends and all."

"Speak, Gerson, what's up?"

"I'm embarrassed to say, but I was a little envious of you and Rosemery. Hell, it's really romantic. Romantic like a Sérgio Reis song."

"Bring the ice bag," Edgar orders, with the kidney in his hands.

Gerson runs to the kitchen, grabs a few ice cubes and takes a thermal bag out of his knapsack. Edgar places the kidney inside, together with two more organs, and zips it shut. They breathe, relieved, and go into the living room.

"Gerson, you'll find a woman who loves you. Now with your kidney back again in place, no one can hold you back, kid," says Edgar, punching Gerson affectionately.

"I think you're right."

Silence. They look at the videotape. They decide to turn off the music and watch the film. Edgar gets two more beers. Gerson looks a little haggard.

"You see how you can't trust anyone anymore, Edgar? My own brother robbed me. Earlier it was dogs eating their owners.

But a relative, a brother, would leave us to the vultures, rotting on the asphalt. The dogs are faithful even when they're devouring us."

"Dogs and Divine Providence bear our greatest burdens," concludes Edgar Wilson.

When they finish the film, the two leave the apartment, but not before going to the bathroom, where the little Chihuahua, with bug-eyes, is rolling in the blood in Marinéia's great open cavity. He chews her robust flesh with tears in his eyes and devours her in tiny bites as if embarked on a long-term ritual or unusually difficult chore.

CHAPTER 3
"Between Dogfights and Hog Slaughter"

Seated behind the steering wheel of the old red truck, Edgar Wilson turns the key in the ignition for the fifth time—and thinks "one-fifth in Hell!"—and is reminded of a story about a one-fifth percent historical tax that collectors would browbeat workers for, "or find them in Hell!" It must have been a hell like today, like this hot and smoldering Thursday.

With his face buried under the hood, Gerson asks Edgar to try one more time. This'll be his sixth attempt, and he remembers the sixth day of the week, Saturday, when he'll be recovering from the dogfights that will have boiled his oxidized blood.

Not a soul passing. They're broken down in the middle of the road.

"Gerson, can it be fixed quickly? The hogs in the bed are going crazy. I can't delay."

"So talk to the boss about getting a decent truck."

Gerson stares off, grimaces with his sweaty face, and smacks his lips to confirm that they're little more than a kilometer from Mr. Abelardo's pigsty.

"Do you think they'll make it?" asks Edgar Wilson.

"I gave them plenty of food today. Taking these pigs for a walk'll do them good," adds Gerson, sure of himself.

An unamused Edgar Wilson comes off the truck, puts on his muddy gloves and thinks his day started complicated. He can appreciate the simplicity of an action, but gets irritated by a decision made without thinking.

He grabs a rope he thinks is sufficiently long, and Gerson makes it his responsibility to tether the animals so they don't come untied during the walk.

"I don't think this one'll be able to keep up with the others. It's still suckling," says Gerson.

"If it can't keep up, I'll carry it," responds Edgar, looking at the sky that has a color he doesn't like, a sickly hue, like the sun when it becomes the color of desperation. He makes the sign of the cross and mutters a short prayer.

"I can't leave the car here."

"But there's no other way, Edgar. We'll hand over the merchandise and from there we'll call a towing service, and see if we can find a mechanic," says Gerson. "We always find a solution."

It's true, he thinks. They always find solutions for any problems that arise. They clip the two ends of the rope, each holding onto one, and take the road, leading six bewildered hogs along the shoulder.

"Desperate, fucking swine. That's why Jesus was a shepherd of sheep," mutters Gerson. "I'd like to see him be a swineherd. These animals show no respect."

Two trucks pass and the pigs run, some to the south and others to the east. For a few seconds they drag the two men, who manage to contain the feverish overexcitement of alarmed animals, unbearable grunting, castration cries.

"The pigs' problem is that they think they're people, like you and me. They look at you and see you as one of them or vice versa," explains Edgar.

"Vice versa, my ass. Nothing in me is like this animal."

"Jesus was a shepherd of sheep, but when the thing went to shit, it was the pigs that took action," says Edgar.

"Must be why it stank. This animal only snores and stinks."

"The thing stank before, don't you remember when Christ had problems with a demon-possessed man and commanded the demons to enter the pigs?"

Edgar gives a dry, brief cough. He feels his lungs complain of the smoke, like it's fogged inside. He needs to quit smoking.

"I don't remember that," says Gerson, tripping occasionally over the rope between his legs.

"They threw themselves into the abyss. They fixed the situation. That's what these animals do, Gerson, they fix things for you," concludes Edgar.

Gerson untangles his legs from the second knot made by the frightened piglet and decides to pick it up to see if he can calm it down. He cradles it in his arms like a baby and then puts it on the ground.

"If that's how it is, Edgar, then tell them to fix the pigsty of a truck."

Edgar stays quiet for a few moments. Stooped. Gerson feels sharp pangs at the height of his kidneys, and a cold sweat sets in, but he doesn't say anything to Edgar. Gerson has kidney disease and in the last few days his urine has contained threads of dehydrated mucus.

"If we had a refrigerated truck we wouldn't need to take this walk with live merchandise," says Gerson. "We could slaughter it all here ourselves and bring it already cut up, and hung on hooks. It'd be marvelous."

Edgar Wilson sees a cigarette ad on a billboard up ahead. It's the same brand he's been smoking for ten years. He exhales until he feels a bit of the smoke inside him dissipate. In ten years, he's never hooked up with a woman as pretty as the one in that ad. Maybe he should smoke more.

"As long as my knife's sharp, I don't mind killing them there," says Edgar, in a hushed tone.

He sighs, and then remembers that his cleaver's still in the car. Well sharpened. He glances back, and the car looks very small in the distance. Too far to return with the hogs, but not so far for a man walking alone.

"Gerson, you go on with them, while I go get my knife."

"Are you sure, Edgar? Can't you use one of Mr. Abelardo's?

He's got dozens in all sizes."

"But none that cuts like mine . . . Not to mention, I've got a way with it, just the right touch."

Edgar's hand fits the handle precisely with an exact edge for slips, and never ever does it hit the steel. It's custom made. It fits his hand perfectly.

Gerson looks at what's at the end of his rope and, rather disappointedly, agrees with his friend. The idea to make the pigs walk was his, and Edgar at no time disagreed. For a friend who makes sacrifices, there's no price. He thinks: we may need to hold the pigs by the tail if necessary, separate the dogs in a fight, but for friends the sacrifices are worth it.

"Can you handle all six?"

Gerson looks at the animals and herds them momentarily in his mind, and says yes, they're just pigs, not war tanks.

Edgar turns and then walks on with purpose. Under this hot sun and on this venomous asphalt path that seems made of asbestos. He keeps an eye fixed on his truck in the distance, and thinks about getting home in time to participate in a new round of dogfights that started recently in a nearby neighborhood and always on Thursdays.

Dogs from Canada against dogs from Bulgaria. He doesn't know where Bulgaria is, but bulldogs must come from there, and in terms of Canada, he can only remember the snow. He saw the snow of Canada in a film, and when he thinks of that whiteness it brings a certain peace of mind and cools his stress. He imagines living in a place like Canada and he suddenly realizes it's the perfect place for someone like him. Someone who gets upset in the heat.

He looks over his shoulder and Gerson gives him the impression of a simple shepherd of sheep at that distance, a sensitive guy with a big heart and goodness. He opens the truck door and sits at the wheel. He turns the key again, and again, with no luck. He gets out of the truck, opens the hood, digs around hoses, tanks, and gizmos for some time and then tries again, the key turns in the ignition, and with a backfire from the exhaust, the truck resuscitates like Lazarus. He slams the hood, checks his cleaver wrapped in a dish towel, and returns to the wheel.

Moments like this bring satisfaction to his life. He's really a man who knows how to solve problems. He pulls out and in one minute catches up to Gerson, stranded on the shoulder between dispersed pigs, with the piglet in his arms. Five meters ahead of them, a car is wrapped around a tree, front end up, hanging on the branches. The car axis and raw wood of the tree form a kind of sculpture, like something very artistic that Gerson once saw in a doctor's home, where he did some electric work. It looked just like this.

"It was in the ignition," says Edgar Wilson, getting out of the truck. "There was a loose wire. I'm surprised you didn't find it, eh, Gerson?"

"Why, Edgar? I didn't find anything wrong with the electrical. Everything was in order."

"That's why Dona Geralda's house caught fire. I always suspected your handiwork in that old lady's house. She died in the electric shower."

"Drop it, the house was haunted. I had nothing to do with it."

Edgar silently inspects the car encrusted on the tree, smoke coming from under the destroyed hood. He scratches his head and dries sweat from his face with his shirtsleeve.

He looks up and sees a ripe mango fall from the tree.

"Just like you said, Edgar, these animals are truly demonized."

Edgar's surprised to remember the animals, and throws himself on the ground to reach the end of the cord before four disoriented hogs, united by a tight knot, escape into the roadside brush.

"It was the piglet. He ran into the road and the car had to swerve," says Gerson. "There's a lady in there."

Edgar scratches his head and looks from one end of the road to the other. There's no sign of another car.

"Help me here first, Gerson. Let's resolve this."

Gerson brings the piglet and Edgar herds the other animals to the truck. He grabs a board to use as a ramp, and the pigs enter noisily.

"One's missing, Gerson."

"Are you sure?"

Edgar serenely looks at the pigs.

"There are only five. The spotted one's not here."

"He must've run to the other side."

"We have to find him. There need to be six."

They hear moaning, an echo intertwined with pauses, and think it must be the escaped pig, possibly injured.

"Did you say there was a lady in there?"

They walk to the car rammed into the tree and through the driver's window, Edgar sees a middle-aged woman disjointed in the metal with some exposed fractures. The woman tries to speak, but can't. From the other side of the car, Gerson picks up a cell phone that's fallen on the ground beneath the passenger seat.

"It's got a signal Edgar."

Edgar asks to see the phone.

"How d'you know?

"Because these little lines rise, see? When they rise like this it's because there's a signal for us to speak," responds Gerson.

Edgar looks at the tiny silver phone, smaller than the palm of his hand. The compact screen has a blue light, blue like the sky is now, and he begins to think it must be a reflection.

"Did you know these play music?"

"No fooling, Gerson."

"Sure thing, Edgar. These are really expensive and even take pictures. I saw one in the store at the mall."

"And when were you ever in a mall, huh, Gerson? You're lying to me."

"I do go. I go to these cool places. Edgar, my life's not only opening pig bellies. I have other interests," says Gerson, getting mad.

Edgar tries to dial a number to ask for help for the woman, but can't remember the number for SOS. 9-1-1 comes to mind, but that's in the United States, here he has no idea. Maybe if he were living in Canada, with all that white snow, he'd know what to dial.

"I also have no idea," responds Gerson.

He decides to call his boss, because he'll know the number for emergencies. Still he's a bit agitated by the loss of the pig, and thinks it best not to show that things have gotten out of hand.

***

Sitting at a table in a kitchen with smudged walls, Zé do Arame hits the numbers on the calculator with thick, truculent, and dirty fingers. Resigned, the poor man laments, to his dog, his lack of resources. He hopes the pigs he sells to Edgar and Gerson will bring enough to keep the lights on at his house.

The dog responds with a solemn moo. He learned to moo with the cows where he grew up, and now he barks and moos according to the occasion.

Zé do Arame puts another spoonful of rattlesnake beans in his mouth and yells:

"Penha, did you put cilantro in the beans again? I can't eat this. It gives me gas."

Penha enters the kitchen carrying a bundle of dirty clothes in one hand, and a freshly killed chicken in the other.

"Those beans give you gas but you insist on eating them," says Penha.

"I was raised on these beans," the man says beating his chest. "I never had gas until you started to cook for me."

He picks up his plate and, after slamming his fist on the table, puts it on the floor for the dog to eat. His wife turns her back, puts the dirty laundry on a chair, and begins to pluck the chicken over the sink.

The phone rings and she asks if he's not going to get it. He orders his wife to get it, and then asks who it is.

"It's Edgar. Says he wants to talk with you."

He gets up and walks to the other room in the small house, pulls up his pants, and answers.

"Speak, Edgar."

"Mr. Zé, do you have the number for succor?"

"Dona Maria de Socorro?

"No. The number we call in the case of emergencies."

"Edgar, are you mixed up in some kind of confusion? What about my hogs, how are they?"

Edgar remains hushed until he can think of something to tell his boss.

"Mr. Zé, there's been an accident on the road and I need to call for help."

"But you should be at Abelardo's by now. He hates delays."

"I know, sir. But we're trying to help."

Mr. Zé listens to the whole story while he picks a piece of bean skin from between his teeth, putting his finger deep into his mouth. He notices that the skin is hard and maybe his wife didn't cook the beans long enough. Maybe this is why he has gas.

"Just a minute, Edgar," he says, and yells to his wife who appears holding the chicken by the neck without stopping to pluck it.

"Oh, Zé, I don't know. Why does Edgar need to know?"

"It's no matter to you, woman. Call Tição, he's out there collecting the offal."

Gerson sits next to the window and decides to talk a little with the lady in agony. She's begun to worry him. He believes his presence can bring her some comfort.

Edgar signals for him to come without dawdling.

"Gerson, what are you doing?"

"Speaking a little with the lady over there."

"Enough chitchat, and go look for the fugitive pig."

Gerson pats down the dust on his pants, crosses the road, and from the other side enters the brush looking for the animal. Zé do Arame comes alive at the other end of the phone line.

"Edgar, Tição's here and he doesn't know. He went to ask a neighbor, who was a security guard."

"I'll wait, Mr. Zé. I'll wait."

He sits back behind the wheel and turns on the radio. There's a lot of static, and then a song that stirs his heart. It's a hit from a telenovela from the 1990s. He can't remember the name, but sings along with the few lyrics he does remember. He looks in the rearview mirror, with the phone still at his ear, and feels like an important somebody. The telephone suits him.

From afar, Gerson signals, disappointed he still hasn't found the pig, and he's going to go deeper into the brush.

"Edgar, son, geez, he's not at home. No one on the street knows the number for succor. There's 9-1-1, right?"

"Yup, in the United States."

"Oh, okay. That's it then," says Zé do Arame. "We probably don't have it here."

Zé do Arame pauses and Edgar doesn't know if he's hung up the phone, until he hears a question on the other end.

"And my pigs, Edgar—are they okay? Come soon because I need money to pay the electric bill today, if not they'll cut it."

"Not if it depends on me. We'll bring the money right away, Mr. Zé. Don't worry."

Edgar pushes some buttons on the screen, and listens with his ear to the phone to make sure he's hung up. He gets out of the truck and goes to the car where the woman is fading. She's got blood in her mouth, spilling out of her ears, and quite a lot running out of her head. He forces the stuck door handle, and with a push makes the car shake, and the woman wakes with a moan. This makes him relax and he waits for her reaction, but she just closes her eyes again.

He walks around the car, thinking about how to remove it from there. He does two half turns and crouches down. He sees a dark puddle beneath the car and thinks it's probably an oil spill, until he confirms it: blood. A big puddle beneath the car.

"Gerson!" Edgar screams, signaling. "I found the fugitive pig."

Gerson crosses the road after an orange Volkswagon Transporter passes. The two men in the van don't notice the car accident, but do see the hogs in the bed of the pickup.

"Where's the bastard?" asks Gerson.

"Down here. We need to get it out," says Edgar. The two men pull the animal with all their strength.

"I think it's stuck on the metal," says Gerson, using brute force.

"Pull harder because it's coming."

And they manage bit-by-bit to drag the pig out from under the vehicle, its body parts dismembered on the ground. They perceive the accident has advanced some of their work, though it'll also complicate things.

"He bought a live pig, Gerson."

"But Edgar, pay attention, we were going to kill it anyway."

"He wants to receive the pig live, understand, Gerson? Mr. Abelardo likes to know his stock, he likes to look the animal in the eye before it dies," says Edgar.

"Okay, and where'll we find another pig, huh? What we should do is tell him about the accident and sell the pig at a discount."

"And who's going to pay the difference? I can't take less money to Mr. Zé, and I'm not going to get stuck with it."

They try to settle down. They're not used to fighting, they never fight, not for anything in the world, and this makes them both feel very uncomfortable.

"And the lady?" asks Gerson.

"She died."

"Poor thing," he pauses. "I was beginning to feel attached."

"No one knows the number for emergencies."

Edgar opens the cell phone. He finds the sound the fragile little tabs make precious.

"You said it plays music, you were lying, right?" asks Edgar.

Gerson's tossing dismembered pork parts into the bed of the pickup and closes the back. He mutters something about the probability of the other pigs eating the dead one, and then they'd be held accountable for an even greater loss.

"They don't like to leave traces," says Edgar Wilson. "That's why they eat anything . . . even themselves," he concludes, as he gets into the truck.

Gerson asks him to wait for a second and tries to empty his bladder. He opens his fly and a dribble of pee falls to the ground; a string of mucus hangs there and he pulls on it with the tip of his finger, ever more worried. He gets in the truck and finds Edgar still amazed by the cell phone.

"It takes pictures too?"

"I'm not well," says Gerson worried. "My piss is drying up."

"And what about that kidney your sister had? Where is it?"

"I left it in the freezer so I could find a fucking doctor to put it back in its place, and my father fried it with onions and ate it while watching an Ipatinga versus Uberlândia soccer match with two of his friends."

"They ate your kidney?"

"That's what I'm saying. I come home and there's the fat, old, stinking goat eating my kidney with onions and having a beer. I thought I'd better not say anything. They thought it was cow's liver. The old man disgusts me, you know."

After a minute of silence and nostalgia, Gerson takes the cell phone from Edgar Wilson's hands. After pressing some buttons he says he's figured it out. He puts his arm around Edgar, who's back on the road, and they take a picture. He shows Edgar the picture of the pair of them on the screen, and Edgar stares.

"If I had one of these, I'd be picking up the ladies all over the place," says Gerson.

"How much do you think it costs?"

"About a thousand bucks, Edgar."

"All that?"

"All that."

"It might cover our losses."

"What an idea, Edgar. Good one."

The telephone rings and on the screen appears the word "husband." Gerson lets it ring and doesn't answer.

"It's the lady's husband," says Gerson.

"How d'you know?"

"It says so here, look . . . H—us—ba—nd."

After a brief, funereal silence, Gerson makes the phone play music, and they're amazed. When they reach Mr. Abelardo's pigsty, they tell him part of the story and he accepts the cell phone in compensation. As the equipment's worth a lot, according to a brother-in-law, they leave the old truck there and drive away in a black pickup ten years younger with shiny tires, plus the exact change for Mr. Zé do Arame to pay his bills.

The boss being satisfied, Edgar Wilson earns an extra commission and bets on the Canadian dog destroying the Bulgarian. He wins, the mangy mutt. And he thinks with a few more dogfights like this one, he could get to know Canada and the white snow.

CHAPTER 4
"Clandestine Butchers and Hogs in the Truck Bed"

"How many can they slaughter?"

"They said thirty in an hour," responds Edgar Wilson, after a long drag on his cigarette.

"Yep . . . never seen anyone break that record," says Gerson, in admiration.

"They say it's the greatest slaughterhouse in the state."

"What's your record, Edgar?"

"Fifteen in an hour."

Gerson slicks back his hair, looks at the waitress passing by, looks at the sway of her butt in ratty jeans. It's plump with many folds and adjacent curves and, this, for Gerson, is a phenomenal ass.

Edgar finishes his coffee and asks for another. Gerson continues to sip his strawberry milkshake through a yellow straw.

"It's twice as many, isn't it?"

"Yes, twice as many and I accept the challenge."

"Edgar Wilson, you're my idol," says Gerson, punching his friend on the shoulder. "What's the prize?"

"The Golden Slaughtered Hog trophy. Mr. Tonico, owner of the largest hog pen in the state, awards it. Who'd have thought it, huh? It's the dream of all butchers . . . fuck . . . what a prize!"

A sweaty, nervous man enters the diner, turns his head from side to side until he sees the back of the place. He moves forward and sits with Edgar and Gerson.

"You must be Edgar Wilson," says the man extending his hand. "And you, Gerson," he greets him next.

The man doesn't stop moving, his fingers drum on the table. He calls the waitress and asks for a shot of cognac with honey. The two just wait for the man to decide to speak.

"So, boys . . . well, you must be wondering . . ."

Gerson interrupts.

"Who told you about us?"

The man looks at Edgar Wilson, who doesn't transmit any emotion in his eyes. He's immutable, sipping his steaming coffee.

"Mr. Chico Maminha . . . the fat baldy . . . from the Maminha do Rei slaughterhouse."

Gerson nods. The man is relieved. He breathes deeply and waits for another question before starting his prepared speech.

"I know it must seem strange for someone to simulate their own abduction, but I need to test my girlfriend's faithfulness . . . Just a minute."

He interrupts himself, grabs his wallet from his pants pocket, and pulls out a photo of his girlfriend.

"This is my girlfriend, Shirlei Márcia. I know it's weird, but before popping the question, I need to be sure . . . really make sure she loves me. She has five thousand reais in an account. It's all of her money . . . if she pays my ransom with the money she's taken years to amass, then I'll know she deserves my love."

Silence.

"You want proof of love?" asks Gerson.

Edgar Wilson is mildly swayed. His girlfriend Rosemery left him a week after Pedro's disappearance. Said she loved Pedro and was going to stay with him. Said she didn't like Edgar Wilson. That she only wanted a new refrigerator.

Rosemery, like Pedro, didn't get very far. Quartered, she was devoured by some hungry hogs at dawn. No remains or traces. He took back the refrigerator with berry magnets.

Edgar sighs, and this makes space in his chest. He should've asked for proof of love from Rosemery. He perfectly understands the man's motives and is overcome by their newfound, shared humanity.

"I just want proof of love. It's guaranteed. I have everything planned. Nothing can go wrong. I'll pay each of you 200 reais, and it shouldn't take more than two hours, max."

Gerson looks at Edgar Wilson waiting for a response, a reaction. He thinks they could ask for more. He values his hourly-fee at a higher rate.

"But we're not kidnappers, and this is crime. We're pork butchers, and there's no crime in that," says Gerson.

"I'm not 'kidnapped,' see? It's only an act."

"Don't know . . . Edgar?"

"I think this man should have his proof of love."

"Do you really?"

"I do," responds Edgar looking at the man. "And I think 200 reais is an acceptable fee for two hours of work. I accept."

"Oh . . . well, then I accept too," says Gerson.

***

On a deserted stretch of road, the man uses a payphone and gesticulates as he speaks. Edgar and Gerson lean against their car, parked by a tree. There's shade. Good shade to lessen the heat. They don't hear what the man says, but they also don't care.

"What did you want to tell me?"

"It's about Pedro."

"That bastard . . . I hope he stays missing forever."

"It's exactly about that . . . about him going missing forever. He was having an affair with Rosemery. I killed them both."

Gerson scratches his head and grimaces with his sweaty face.

"He got what he deserved then. Don't worry, Edgar, he was a good for nothing."

"I'm not worried."

"I'd do the same. I'd kill them and slop the hogs their remains."

"I threw them in like swill and they ate all of it."

"Starving beasts . . ."

Silence.

"You redeemed your honor," says Gerson, inspired to give Edgar Wilson a hug. "Did you take back the refrigerator?"

"I did and am paying it off in installments."

"That fridge is a real beaut."

"It makes ice on medium," comments Edgar.

"Mine's a mess. It doesn't work in this heat."

"If you need ice you can get it from mine. There's space in it too. You can use it whenever you like."

Gerson looks at his friend, softened. Only someone who lives in the confines of the stuffy and suffocating 100-degree suburbs, far from the beaches, from humid sea breezes, swallowing dust, saving water, stepping on steaming asphalt every day, knows what a new, ice-making refrigerator means. Around here, it's worth gold. Just like treated water and closed sewers, but unfortunately they still have to live with open-air shit and worms.

The man returns animated and a little nervous. The time is now. No one knows about the simulated kidnapping, except Mr. Chico Maminha, who's completely trustworthy. The man hands over a piece of paper with the name and number of his fiancée, the exact value to be demanded in ransom, and a short text to be read aloud. How little each of them can read worries him, but they'll figure it out.

The man is tied up, wrists and ankles cuffed. Total realism is necessary. He asks them to punch him. With a little blood on his face and some bruises, it'll be even more convincing. Gerson socks him twice. It's enough for blood to run.

They put their kidnap victim in the trunk of his own brown Fiat Uno. They slam the door with force, turn half around, get in the same car and squeal out with the sound system on.

"What's his name again?"

"I don't remember, Edgar. I don't think he said."

Gerson gets the note with his annotations. He checks but doesn't find any name except Shirlei Márcia. Gerson lowers the volume on the radio and yells in the direction of the trunk for the man's name. He hears a muffled groan in response.

"What is it?" he yells again.

Edgar Wilson shakes his head and squints.

"Gerson, I think it's Cleiton."

"No, he said Heraldo."

"Of course not. It was nothing like that. It's Cleiton."

"I'm sure I heard Heraldo. Yes, it's Heraldo. I heard him."

Edgar could deny it once more, but the man's name didn't matter very much just then. They'd ask later. There was time for this and time to eat something.

Dona Elza's Mandioca Frita, the faded sign evokes the image of a robust Northeasterner with a manioc root in her hand. A good place to eat: prices that don't empty pockets, and plates that always fill the stomach. A deal only found at *Dona Elza's Mandioca Frita,* and so they stop to eat. They park the car between two heavy-load trucks; the place caters to truckers and travelers. Space to eat, take a nap, and fuck. Dona Elza also serves up this kind of pleasure. She manages yuca and yaya with dexterity and aptitude. The dish of the day is accompanied by forty-year-old cunt. Specials like that; only here.

They climb out of the car, slam doors, and walk to the restaurant. The owner receives them with open arms.

***

A little while later, Edgar Wilson is disputing flies over the last pork rib with fried yuca on a tray on the table. Now and then he feels a warm breeze from a swinging wall fan that turns slowly and groans in agony.

Gerson returns from the bathroom and sits back down at the table. Edgar finishes eating the last rib and they go to the cash register.

"You bought two specials. Will you want to fuck?"

"Who fucks in heat like this? With one of these cunts?" Gerson asks the boy behind the register.

"Can we exchange the cunt for one of those ice creams?" asks Edgar pointing to the freezer.

The boy flips his cap around and looks at the owner.

"I need to speak with Dona Elza. Are you sure? You'd prefer ice cream?"

"Absolutely," responds Gerson.

In opening the restaurant door, the dry, hot gust of air softens their ice cream. Bowls with half a kilo of Neapolitan flavor. They lean on a railing and enjoy their desserts.

"I'd trade three fifteen-year-old pussies for this," says Gerson. "Who fucks in this heat?"

"Only pigs."

He watches a truck maneuver a heavy load. The driver has had more than a few. His eyes are red, his face is droopy, and he's probably got the taste of old yaya in his mouth. He attempts a number of times to nose out of a space, but breaks too quickly; the motor goes quiet. He seems confused. The two continue to eat their ice creams, which are already the consistency of soup.

After a quiet moment, truck and driver decide to pull out of the parking spot once and for all, and that's when he slams into the back of the brown Fiat Uno. The car plunges forward a few meters and the truck takes off for the open road. He finally got it in gear after banging up the rear end of their car.

Gerson and Edgar go to the car and with difficulty suspend the trunk door.

"Now we'll never know his name," says Gerson.

Edgar slams the trunk shut, and gets into the car, followed by Gerson, and they leave.

Now he'll never have his proof of love, is what Edgar Wilson thinks. Gerson picks up the note with annotations made by the man, tears it up, and throws it out the window. The car's struggling on its journey since it's quite damaged and after two kilometers it begins to smoke under the hood.

They get out of the car and Edgar Wilson finds comfort as he admires a large leafy tree throwing wide and generous shade. On the other side of the road, there's a public phone.

"We're close to Dona Maria das Vacas's pigsty," says Gerson. "Doesn't her son own a junkyard?"

"He does."

"So we can leave the car with him, and the guy in it . . . I mean . . ."

"Slop to the pigs," finished Edgar.

"That's it."

Gerson walks to the public phone, which isn't working.

"One of us'll have to go there."

Gerson turns the dead man over in the trunk, grabs the license from his wallet, and reads his name there.

"It's Cleiton, his name. Shocking how good you are, Edgar Wilson. Shocking."

They walk five hundred meters to the junkyard. Dona Maria das Vacas's son is lunching on a fried egg and two tinned sardines. They tell him about the car, the accident, and all three get into a tow truck.

"I'd never ask something like that of my wife, Rosinete . . . ha . . . daughterofabitch'd let me rot," says the man, driving, and he bursts out laughing. "She'd run away with the first guy she meets, sell my junk, and send my kids to an institute. Proof of love, who needs it? What shit."

They get off at the site, tow the truck, and leave the body in Dona Maria das Vacas's hog pen.

"These animals will eat anything and . . . anything," says the man throwing the body to the hogs. "And they never leave a trace," he adds, laughing, satisfied.

"That's what I always say," Edgar agrees.

And the sound of voraciously crunching bones reverberates between ravenous snorts.

"I was raised in this hog pen, but I'm still impressed watching these brutes feed," says the man, and the three sit quietly for some time.

They lost a day of work. As payment for the favor, they leave the car in the junkyard. It was their loss that they didn't kill pigs that day, but at least it was resolved in the end.

***

The next day, Edgar Wilson stands beside other butchers and before dozens of pigs. The swine are agitated and helplessly entangled. Holding his sharpened blade, the handle of which perfectly fits his hand, he begins his slaughtering as soon as the shot's fired. He feels nervous at first, but has a pretty good crowd. And who knew that between dogfights and slaughtered hogs he'd kill thirty-three, breaking the state's record. Thirty-three is the age of Christ when he died. Thirty-three is the age he reached last year. He looks up at the sky and Divine Providence gives her sign once more.

Edgar Wilson is the new record-holder. He wins the Slaughtered Hog trophy and a good sum of money. He never thought, never imagined that his ways and efforts would make him a winner. And life is really very good, he thinks.

CHAPTER 5
"Pigs Can't Look Up at the Sky"

A fighting dog is a dog that has no choice. He learned what his owner chose to teach him ever since he was a puppy. He's recognizable by his short or amputated ears, scars, stitches, and lacerations. He's had no choices in life. That's exactly how it's been for Edgar Wilson who was trained at a young age to kill rabbits and frogs. He has some scars beneath his arms, and on his neck and chest. There are so many lines and sutures on his skin he doesn't remember where he got half of them. However, scars of violence and resistance to death on other animals have never dulled the glint in his eye while he contemplates a big sky. Night and day, he spends a good deal of time looking up. Maybe he expects something to happen in the sky or with the sky . . . maybe he'd like to cut up some clouds with his big knife.

Despite having been raised like a fighting dog, he knows it's better than being a pig. That's because pigs can't look up at the sky. They just can't. Anatomically, pigs were made basically to look at the ground and to feed on whatever they found there. Edgar knows that he's a fighting dog raised to kill pigs, rabbits, and men. However, every bit of a pig is relished. Rabbits can be eaten with green olives and almonds. Men are often given a mass. As an excuse to light a candle and pray.

Tonight's blood fight will be between Chacal and a new dog, a Dogo Argentino, called Eclipse. His name describes his ability to become nearly invisible to other dogs, finding his adversary's vulnerability in its shadow. And it's in the shadows that he attacks and devours. He was born on a hot night, when the moon hid behind clouds. Although, minutes later the moon appeared again, lacerated in the sky.

"Who'll you bet on, Edgar?"

"On the bastard Chacal," he responds.

"I don't know. The other one hides in the shadows, that's what they say."

"Gerson, I saw this dog's birth. I knew the wretched beast before he opened his eyes."

"I know, Edgar. I know."

"Sly as a fox, and violent as a wolf, Chacal's the worst monster I've seen in life. So bad, he has no shadow. The Dogo Argentino doesn't stand a chance."

"I'm going to bet on Eclipse," says Gerson. "I'm going to put all my money on the Argentine sonofabitch."

"You know best. In addition to being a fighting dog, he's Argentine," says Edgar Wilson.

"That makes him twice as wretched," returns Gerson.

"You're right. But I'll say it again—Chacal has no shadow. He leaves no trace. I'll bet on him so long as he's in fighting condition."

Edgar Wilson puts out his cigarette and gets up from the curb. He cracks his fingers and adjusts his cap, because he knows it's time to go to the back, to the knacker's yard. He calls the clandestine slaughterhouse a knackery because it's a cut-and-cover for dismantling animals. He's worked in a mechanics shop, and as cars came in they were dismantled, hung on hooks on the walls, and put on shelves. And parts were sold separately.

He leaves the fattest hogs to day's end. The sun at the end of the day always brings respite, a necessary repose, since it's three-times the effort to work such fatty meat and three-times the sweat.

Gerson grinds his knife blade against the curb to make it sharp. He likes to impress the neighborhood girls who bat their lashes when the sparks fly. A pang at the height of his kidney makes him suddenly dizzy. He's been passing mucus in his urine lately, and toward the end of the day he feels more pain. But at day's end he should feel better: it's happy hour, time to play billiards and shoot the shit at Cristóvão's bar.

The laborer's day ends when the sun goes down. That's when Gerson and Edgar Wilson get their recompense. A respite from the sun. A job accomplished. They feel welcome to enjoy life's simple and practical pleasures.

A bald-tired vehicle riddled with bullet holes pulls up and parks on the other side of the dusty road. It's odd to see police around here. It's not like anyone's died or anything. That's to say, they haven't heard of any fatal accident, or failed robbery, or anything like that. Generally when police appear, when they come out this way, it's because someone's already dead. They'll come out to write a report, have a coffee while they wait for a hearse, and go off again. Here, they rarely save a life. It was just too far, no one knew how to get here, they got lost along the way. That's how they justify arriving too late on the scene. That's why every citizen has a big knife, whether it's sharp or not. The police arrive when it's time to write up the occurrence and some pertinent facts concerning the deceased. It's simpler to deal with the dead. Write up a report, open an investigation, and go home for dinner. Here, there's also dinner. At least here, death doesn't take away an appetite. They've dealt with it from youth. The manholes have no covers here, but are exposed, and only the careless fall down. This is how it is, here.

"Good afternoon."

"Good afternoon."

"Good afternoon."

"Good afternoon."

"Boys, do you have a glass of water for us?" asks the senior policeman, an elderly sort.

"Of course," says Gerson.

"Has something happened?" Edgar wants to know.

"That's right, boy. Something's happened," responds the

police officer.

"Can we help?" asks Gerson.

"You can. Bring that water to begin."

Gerson runs to the knackery and returns with water. While they wait, Edgar doesn't say a word. The policeman either. Then, the old man drinks water and clicks his tongue in satisfaction.

"Water around here is worth gold, no?" he says.

"That's what my friend here, Edgar, always says," responds Gerson.

"You are Edgar Wilson and Gerson Batista, are you not?" he asks.

"Yes, sir. Something wrong?" says Gerson.

The other, much younger, policeman is mute. He's seriously attentive to the conversation.

"Well, there's always something or other that's not quite right, let's just say. And we have a little problem here that's quite irritating." He takes a look at the notebook he's just taken from his pocket. "Do you boys know a Cleiton Aparecido de Jesus?"

Gerson puts his cleaver in his belt and covers it with his shirt. Edgar swats at flies. They seem to smell the odor of his soul.

"I can't remember," says Gerson.

"And you?" he asks Edgar.

"Also negative, sir."

The policeman scratches his head a bit. Then he scratches his beard. Then he pulls up his pants. The pants are tight. The excess belly fat makes Edgar sigh about how much work awaits him out back. Three immense hogs are back there—still alive. He sighs again.

"He disappeared a few days ago and was seen with you two."

"Did he work with pigs?" asks Gerson.

"He was a civil servant. He worked in an office in the city center."

"I never met anyone who works in public office," mutters Gerson.

"What about you, Edgar?"

He shakes his head, then lights a cigarette.

"Are you sure this guy was seen with us?" Gerson prods.

"Certain. They identified you at a bar two kilometers from here. He had a brown Fiat Uno, which also disappeared," replies the officer, wiping sweat from his forehead with an index finger. A small puddle drops on the ground.

"I know," says Gerson.

The four are silent for a while. A truck approaches and, before leaving them in its dust, the driver yells for Edgar Wilson to pick up his pig within two hours, giving no time for him to answer.

"You guys seem to have a lot of work," says the cop.

"We do. We butcher hogs. Every day," says Gerson, who then points to the other cop with a nod of his head and asks, "Doesn't he talk?"

"He can't speak. He was injured during a police operation and left mute. But he's an excellent officer, even without an active voice," he responds.

He looks at his friend and gives him a pat on his left shoulder. The old man seems like a satisfied guy. Really always satisfied. Gerson finds it odd. An old pig on the streets with a much younger, mute cop. What are mute cops good for? And the response comes immediately, as if his thoughts have been read.

"It's better to be silent. For a police officer, being mute is essential. After all, who listens in this day and age?" he says and utters a bray-like chuckle. He clears his throat, spits on the ground, and concentrates. "Are you guys certain you've really never seen this guy?"

"Officer, I don't remember the guy. But Edgar, here, and me, we meet all sorts all the time. You must not know this, sir, working with pigs requires a lot from us . . . that thing of . . . you know, sir, . . . net . . ."

"Sociability," the police officer finishes.

"That's it. We've got a lot of that. We're here and there, and when we pay attention, we're already somewhere else, unloading pigs or finding new pigsties. And also . . . keeping up to date with the techniques," concludes Gerson.

Edgar Wilson has finished his cigarette. He's sufficiently irritated by the conversation and now he's running late. He puts his cigarette out in the small puddle of sweat dashed on the ground by the old man, and decides to speak up.

"Maybe he decided to split?"

In saying this, Edgar Wilson feels a strong urge to go home and prepare for tonight's dogfight. He feels like slaughtering hogs only tomorrow, but knows this is impossible. He needs to meet his obligations.

"Sometimes I feel like skipping town," sighs Gerson. "I'd like to know if anyone would go looking for me."

The policeman writes something in his notebook, clears his throat again, and spits on the ground.

"We've not discarded any possibility," says the cop. "We do our work competently."

Gerson removes the knife from his belt and feels a pang at the height of his kidney. His urine is pure mucus. He wonders how much longer he'll stay alive with just the one kidney. His hemodialysis sessions have become daily events and his earnings at work have diminished. If it weren't for Edgar Wilson and his friendship, Gerson would've become unemployed long ago. Edgar's been doing the work of two without complaint. He knows what it means to be a friend and makes sacrifices accordingly.

Edgar Wilson puts on the pair of rubber gloves hanging from his back pocket. They stand side by side. Very serious. The older police officer doesn't know what to do. Gerson speaks cautiously.

"I had a cousin who disappeared. He left for work one day and never came home. Ten years later, they discovered he was living in Pará, happy as ever. The bastard left debt for my aunt to pay . . . that's why she became a hooker. She needed to pay his debts and feed five children. She sucked so much dick that when she died she didn't have a tooth left in her mouth."

No one speaks. The flies buzz around their heads. Large, disgusting flies. Edgar Wilson takes the cigarette pack out of his pocket. His last cigarette is on the ground, extinguished in the policeman's sweat. He crumples the pack and throws it over his left shoulder. On sunny days like these, with stagnant air, smelling of sewage, and tripe stuck deep up his nose, he sometimes feels it will never end. He feels condemned to this place, to this situation. The stench and heat restrict his movements and complicate his thinking. All he can do is wait for nighttime's more tolerable temperature and occasional breeze.

"Okay, then," says the policeman. "Edgar Wilson and Gerson, thanks for your attention and your help. I won't take any more of your time, boys. I see you're fine, hardworking folk."

"You're welcome," says Gerson, and Edgar Wilson nods politely.

The police officers walk to the other side of the road. They climb into their vehicle and disappear around the corner. After breathing the dust left by the car, Edgar and Gerson go into the knackery.

"Suppose it's the guy from the kidnapping, Edgar?"

"Could be."

"Do you remember his name?"

"I can't remember his face."

"Fuck him. The cop said it, we're good and hardworking."

"That's right, Gerson. That's right. Now, hold that beast."

Edgar Wilson strikes a single blow with a club to the hog's head. It's only got time for a grunt before another blow is struck. It falls, dying, and the second in line is dragged to slaughter. Edgar dries the sweat from his forehead, grabs another pack of cigarettes from behind the deli counter, lights one and continues clubbing hogs. "We're fine, hardworking folk," is what he thinks when he singes one of the hogs until its hide crackles, and then he slits it open from one end to the other.

***

HFAC – Humane Farm Animal Care Standards for Pigs

1. *Pigs must be frequently and considerately handled by the caretakers to reduce fear and improve welfare and management.*
2. *Caretakers must be able to demonstrate competence in handling animals in a positive and compassionate manner.*

"Positive and compassionate," mutters Edgar Wilson, as he reads these standards nailed to the knackery wall. He works so hard he usually has no time to read notices posted on that wall. This one's already yellowing and he doesn't remember seeing it before. Blocking other items of the care of pigs established by the Humane Farm Animal Care, he reads the pamphlet that announces canary fights. He's never been to one and he knows they're induced to fight over a female, but the winner doesn't get to keep the bait. It's prepped for the next fight. "Terrible for the canaries," thinks Edgar. His sex life is about as good as that of a fighting canary. It's been too much work and too little reward.

He leaves his rubber gloves on the counter, pulls a cigarette from behind his ear and puts it in his mouth. He's out of matches. Gerson enters the office and leaves some new hooks on the floor.

"This kidney's killing me," Gerson complains.

"Or the absence of it is," responds Edgar.

Gerson grabs a tin cup and pours coffee from a thermos.

"The hemodialysis sessions are killing me. I'm not going to survive this very much longer."

The money was always meager, now it's scarce. Gerson works on his boss's compassion and his friend Edgar Wilson's loyalty. His meager earnings go into kidney treatment. He also spends a lot on bus fare. He takes two to get to the hospital and two to return. He eats poorly. Sleeps poorly. He knows he'll soon die. Somehow he simply knows this. There's no one in the world who matters to him, aside from Edgar Wilson. Gerson suffers from chronic kidney disease, and he suspects that from one minute to the next it'll just stop functioning. He takes another sip of coffee and goes to the bathroom. He feels tremendous burning, his entrails flare up, and he pisses blood. Edgar sighs hearing his groans.

"You know something, Edgar?"

"I know some things."

"But this one I don't think you know."

"So what is it, Gerson?"

"I'm dying."

"No, not that."

"Yes, I am. Edgar Wilson, I'm dying. I'm pissing so much blood, I'm anemic, I purge almost every day, I'm practically skin and bone. I can't kill pigs right. I'm in pain all the time."

"You're very much alive, Gerson. You're here!"

"I only get in your way, Edgar. You work twice as hard on my account."

Gerson shuts up. He lowers his head. They're quiet for a second.

"What can I hope for in this life, Edgar? What can I expect from these doctors? These hospitals? I'm going to bleed to death . . . I'll die in some hospital corridor, Edgar."

Edgar Wilson lights the cigarette that's been hanging between his lips for some time. The burst from the match almost breaks up their conversation. He throws the used match on the ground.

"I'm only a hog slaughterer. I don't have a chance. I won't die in some hospital corridor," says Gerson, and then he breaks into a half smirk, behind which he tries to hide. "We've enjoyed life, haven't we?"

Edgar doesn't respond.

"I don't want this for me, Edgar. I don't want it. You're the only one I've got in life and I know I won't have anyone else ever. When I gave my kidney to my sister Marineía, I thought I was doing good. I thought she'd like me for it. I thought the family would treat me like a hero."

He gulps down the rest of his coffee. His eyes are swollen and a bit teary.

"They're wretched people, Gerson. You're the only one worth a damn in that family, my friend."

Gerson titters nervously. He approaches Edgar and gives him a quick hug. They're too tough to hold an embrace.

"Will you put money on the Dogo Argentino tonight?" Edgar Wilson inquires.

"I will. And he'll win from the bastard Chacal," responds Gerson with a smile. "We're going to have a good time tonight."

"You'll be damned tonight," says Edgar.

***

Chewing gum stretches between the small stadium seats and the seat of Edgar Wilson's pants when he stands up to go buy another beer. He doesn't notice the Chiclets attached to the seat of his pants, but sees the Dogo Argentino bets rising even before the fight begins. He likes to lay eyes on the dog before a fight. He approaches Chacal, and the dog looks back at Edgar Wilson and howls.

He returns to his place, hands Gerson a beer, and remarks, upset:

"Chacal doesn't seem well to me."

"Did you go see the pest?"

"I took a peek. I didn't like what I saw."

"What was it?

"Something in the eye of that beast tells me he won't get through the day. And he knows it."

"I bet everything on Dogo Argentino."

"I'm putting my money on Chacal to win."

"Even knowing he'll lose, Edgar?"

"I'm loyal to the dog."

"Even knowing he won't get through today?"

"Even so. Until death."

Someone chucks a beer can and hits Edgar Wilson on the head. It's the second time tonight that this most repugnant, sordid crowd manifests enthusiasm.

"Going to break his face?" asks Gerson.

"No. His neck."

Edgar gets up and walks over to the man who chucked the beer can. He raises him up by the neck and throws him into the horse trough. The audience vibrates more and he almost brings the house down. They like to see Edgar involved in ritualized combat, which is rare, except for certain provocations. They applaud Edgar, who returns to his bench.

There were people from everywhere. Trucks, wagons, bicycles, motorcycles, and cars piled up in front of the Tanganica junkyard. Even Tanganica himself wandered among the crowd. The short, brown man greeted and collected bet money while sucking a toothpick between four remaining teeth. He smelled of pine, and no one understood why. He was always grimy, chewing on a toothpick, and smelling of pine.

The blood fight in the small arena was over. Neither had been killed, the owner didn't allow it, he thought he could still make some money on the unfortunate dog, even all cut up. Just dress the lacerations and he'd be good for more fights.

Pulled by his leather collar into the pit by his owner, Tanganica, Chacal is muzzled. He grunts like a pig. Edgar is somewhat apprehensive. He steps away from the crowd and seeks a place high in the stands. He looks at the sky; the moon is hidden. He searches all ends of the sky as far as his eye can see, there's no trace of it at all.

Chacal's a star, the old regulars' favorite, and this'll be his last. Born to fight, he'll die fighting. He'll fight to the last breath.

Gerson anxiously sits perched in his seat. In pain, breathing heavily, he lets out a cry of courage.

They bring in the Dogo Argentino. Eclipse trots into the pit, muzzled, and pulled on a rope. Chacal stirs. The owners face their dogs, pull off muzzles and release the collars. Instantaneously the dogs hurdle and clash in the air with fury. As the smell of dogs' blood drenches the ground soil, their fury grows. It isn't a fight, but a duel. The Dogo Argentino is younger than Chacal, has the strength of a horse, and the speed of a leopard. Edgar Wilson knows he's lost all his money on this bet, has known it from the start. The dog entered the arena to die, to die a hero. Gerson, leaning over the pit, vibrates with his imminent victory. Edgar Wilson doesn't see the fatal blow when it's delivered to Chacal. He's looking at the sky. For seconds, he contemplates its immensity and follows the movement of clouds, which gradually allow the moon to appear.

Sad days can be cold or hot, gray or blue. And shadows contour souls, desires, and thoughts. These shadows belong to no one, they can come from anywhere: from a wall nearby, an ocean wave, an expanded wing in the sky. Sometimes, even the stars seem to make shadows. Though they're dead, they overshadow with their insistent glimpse of infinity. And in thinking of stars, sometimes he wishes for a stairway to the sky. So he can blow them out.

When he looks back at the pit, Tanganica is carrying Chacal out in pieces. He takes the dog out behind the junkyard where he'll bury it, put up a wooden cross with its name and date of birth, next to five other crosses for five other dogs. And, there's still plenty of room for new dogs and new sacrifices.

***

On their way home, along a deserted path between trees and dry bushes, Gerson and Edgar are uncommunicative. They've had a difficult night. But what's done is done. Gerson stands next to a tree, puts his beer on the ground, and urinates painfully. He gasps when he pulls up his fly. After he's finished, he stands still in place. Edgar waits, patiently. He comes back minutes later without the beer.

"Is it worse, Gerson?" asks Edgar.

He nods. He's sweating more than usual. He inhales deeply. He advances like he's going to purge, one hand over his mouth, but holds back his rising intestines. He begins to walk like he might keel over. He utters a strange guffaw. His legs twist and he falls to the ground convulsing. He's taken poison. Edgar kneels and holds the man's body.

"I beat you, didn't I, Edgar?"

Edgar sits on the ground and supports his friend's head against his chest. He embraces it and says:

"Yes, you won, you motherfucker."

Gerson convulses and struggles with the urge to speak.

"What'll you do with the money I won, Edgar?"

"I'll bury you."

Gerson cracks up.

"Go on a trip. I never traveled."

"Where should I go?"

"See snow."

"That's very far."

"I won big. Sell the refrigerator, you won't need it anymore."

"No, I won't."

"Promise me you'll see snow."

"I promise I'll find some wretched snow."

And he says no more. Edgar doesn't know what to do, so he remains there embracing Gerson's body until dawn. When dawn comes, the sun doesn't shine. The day is cloudy with frequent showers. Edgar doesn't go to work. It's his day off. He sells his new refrigerator and a few other objects of value, and adds this to the good sum that Gerson won in the fight, along with the savings he keeps hidden in a tin of buttered biscuits. He throws a rucksack on his back and finds the nearest highway. He walks a long way to get there. He hitches a ride on a southbound truck. He'll head south. He'll cross the country, cross borders until he finds snow. Any snow.

BOOK 2. “The Dirty Work of Others”

Plague went before him; pestilence followed his steps.

— Habakkuk 3:5

CHAPTER 1

There's trash everywhere, of every variety: atomic, spatial, special, hospital, industrial, radioactive, organic, and inorganic, but Erasmo Wagner only knows one kind. It's household trash. What's filthy, rotten, sour, and has gone bad. What's of no use to anyone but vultures, rats, dogs, and people like him. He generally works days on a garbage truck with alternating shifts at night. He knows what a bag contains just by its smell, shape, and heft. He's had tetanus. He's had tuberculosis. He's been bitten by rats and pecked at by vultures. He knows pests, fear, and horror; that's why he's perfect for the job.

He takes home, to resell, what he finds in decent shape: mattress, bedpost, toilet, door, dresser, fence, safe, chair, pipe, or whatever might be usable. He complements his salary by half with junk sales.

He doesn't consider the wretched landfill scavengers, who could also benefit from the better trash. He just doesn't care. Just as those above him don't care. In the diminishing scale from starving to degenerate, he occupies a place just above miserable. Missing it just by a hair, same as being grazed by a bullet.

Erasmo Wagner picks up more than twenty tons of garbage on his daily route. Measures the wealth of a society by the amount of trash it produces. And his is a fairly short route, so he thinks about how much money goes into what ends up being thrown out. Everything transforms into trash; even he himself is trash to the many people, rats, and vultures that constantly peck at him.

It doesn't bother him. They're acting on instinct. His rotten stench gets to them, and they attack. The others, fellow scavengers, don't advance, but rather stand as far away as they can, as far away as they do from the debris and toxic remains from their homes. The smell of him keeps people at a distance.

His life isn't just garbage. It's really garbage. Nostrils full of rot. His odor is sour; his nails blackened; his beard wiry, ratty, and spotty. No one likes Erasmo Wagner very much. They walk away from him when he's working, and he prefers it that way. He prefers vultures, rats, and filth; that's what he knows. It's what sustains him. People, generally, make him want to barf.

His girlfriend, Suzete, doesn't mind him. Suzete cleans public bathrooms for a living. She smells of piss, shit, and Pine-Sol.

"What do you mean they extended the route?" Erasmo Wagner, soaked in rain, yells to the garbage truck driver.

"We'll be covering two more blocks," the driver replies.

"Why?"

"A truck broke down. We need to finish the collection."

Erasmo Wagner doesn't like doing other people's dirty work. He hoists two more bags into the back of the truck, activates the compactor, and swings himself onto the tailgate. He grabs onto a steel rail for support. He's used to holding on. Standing like that, he's able to catch a little shuteye, even on tight curves.

"We collect the extra trash but won't get paid for it right?" asks Valtair, the rookie collector.

"You bet. We should be earning by the ton. What's worse, there's always extra trash."

The noisy truck stops five blocks ahead, and they start collecting the extra garbage.

"I don't like rich people's streets," says Erasmo Wagner. "So much more trash."

"They have cash to throw away, that's all," Valtair responds.

The rain came down heavier in the last few minutes. It grew darker. Dreary mid-afternoon. They pull on their black plastic capes. They look like merchants of death, collecting black bags and dumping the disgusting contents of trash bins directly into the compactor or, as they call it, the "crusher."

"Money always becomes trash. Trash is crap," says Erasmo Wagner. "My cousin, Edivardes, unclogs sewers for a living. Shit labor, for sure. You need to see rich people's sewage. He says it's denser."

Erasmo Wagner hustles for a large, over-full bag that's fallen in the middle of the street. He kicks a mutt that's snapped up a chicken head. The animal growls and runs off, holding on to the rotten meat. Erasmo Wagner throws the bag into the crusher.

"Heavy shit?" asks Valtair, rolling a garbage can.

"Yes. Concentrated. Good food does that. Poor people's shit is lean and watery. Edivardes knows people by the shit they produce. He doesn't miss a thing. He's street savvy."

They cross from one side of the street to the other, collecting large and small bags. Sometimes they fight for the garbage they need to collect, kicking aside a dog or trading slaps with beggars scrounging for food. Valtair stands by as one boy scavenges a bag. Erasmo Wagner pulls the bag away and throws it into the truck. Valtair feels desolate.

"A week from now, you'll be treating everyone the same—dogs and beggars," says Erasmo Wagner. "The rot does that. Pretty soon the only sense you'll have left will be smell."

Erasmo Wagner bends over to pull a piece of feces-covered newspaper from his boot. The rain remains heavy. It's muggy. The trash is more acrid than normal.

"You can't wait on dogs and beggars," he says. "They fuck with our work. Spread food everywhere. Make a mess of everything."

"Hurry up back there!" the garbage truck driver yells from the cab. Erasmo Wagner doesn't like this driver. He's an abominable guy who doesn't like detritus. All he wants to do is drive and smoke. He lights a cigarette and eats half a bowl of *Angu `a Bahaiana* polenta seated at the steering wheel, while they run back and forth, with no respite, under heavy rain. The cab is for the driver. The tailgate attached to the rear of the truck is for the collector. No matter the weather, makes no difference; there he is, balancing on the tailgate, holding onto an iron bar or some rope. At this job, the only thing that matters is collecting trash and respecting the hierarchy.

The truck they work on doesn't have a semiautomatic pick-up system. They really have to get their hands dirty. There are all sorts of risks. But there's risk everywhere.

After a run, Valtair returns with an antler of branches. "You can't put that in there," says Erasmo Wagner. "The other guys get that. We just pick up the stuff in bags. Branches can jam the crusher."

Finishing the extra collection, they jump onto the tailgate. Standing on the running board, they're bumped about until they get back to the yard. That's about twenty minutes straight. Plenty of time to think about life. Twenty minutes extend into nearly an hour. Traffic is slow all over the city because of the rain. Shit seeps from sewers, and asphalt is breaking up—means more dirt the next day.

From across the street, in the middle of traffic, they hear shouts and snarls. An old man is being attacked by a pit bull, fierce as a fighting dog. The old man falls to the ground and they run over to help him. Valtair tries to pry the animal away with a stick. But this only makes it madder. The truck driver watches from his rearview mirror. He opens the cab door and climbs out. He falls over and picks himself back up again. The dog's jaws go to snap the old man's neck. The old man defends himself. Valtair shouts to scare the dog.

Erasmo Wagner just watches the scene. He was bit by a dog when he was a kid. An old man beat him with a stick when he was a kid, for stealing two oranges. He was hungry, and not strong or big enough to work, or to defend himself, either from the dog or the old man.

It makes little difference to him who survives. The dog will likely rip the old man apart. Old men have thin skin. He knows it. He's killed one too. But it was a long time ago, and the old man was no good. Erasmo Wagner's paid for it, and now he's free to collect all the trash in the world, if that's what it takes. Prison taught him to appreciate the discarded stuff.

Valtair is on the verge of tears. If Erasmo doesn't do something, no one will. He cracks his knuckles and takes a pocketknife from his jacket. He jumps the dog and digs the knife into its neck. The dog doesn't seem to feel a thing. Fury anaesthetizes the body. Erasmo Wagner knows this too. He pulls the dog against his own weight and they roll on the ground. He yells for the driver to start the crusher.

Erasmo Wagner is a brute. Before collecting trash, he broke asphalt with a jackhammer, six hours a day. He broke up asphalt for more than thirty kilometers under scalding sun. It's been a while since he's had a fight, since he's chosen to defend someone other than himself.

The driver drags his enormous belly back into the truck. Erasmo Wagner hugs the dog from behind. He runs to the truck. The crusher is ready to chew the dog's flesh and bones. He throws the dog inside and manages to pull his favorite pocketknife from the wild beast's neck just before the compactor pulls him in. Pieces of dog are devoured and regurgitated. Blood and innards splatter Erasmo Wagner. He cleans his face with the back of his hand. The beast's entrails smell of carnage. Now, Erasmo Wagner will have to take special care not to become prey to rats and vultures.

Valtair helps the old man to his feet. He's not badly hurt. Someone calls a policeman from a nearby precinct. The dog's owner appears. He wants to know where his dog is. Erasmo Wagner shows him what's in the crusher. The young man bends over and vomits açai with granola. He wants to be indemnified. He wants to argue.

"Do you know who you're talking to," he asks.

"I know your garbage," Erasmo Wagner responds. "I know who I'm talking to."

He says this and appears to be bigger than he is. Furious and bloodied, he becomes frightening. The young man quiets down. The policeman wants to take everyone to the station.

"I still have work to do," Erasmo Wagner says.

"Let's all go to the station," says the policeman. "All of you, and the truck, because the perpetrator's inside the truck, right? So I have to take all of you to the station."

"He's in the crusher," Valtair says.

"We'll take what's left as is."

Hours later, they're free to go. The dog's mortal remains are to be recovered by its owner when they arrive at the dump. Chief's orders. The dog has a right to a funeral. The old man tries to tip Erasmo Wagner 500 reais. He refuses. He sees him off and jumps on the back of the truck with Valtair. It's been a long day. The rain stopped a while ago. The night is muggy. Everyone's exhausted and starving.

"I still don't know how you managed to throw that dog into the truck."

"I hate dogs, Valtair. I hate everything almost all the time."

"Why?"

"I don't know."

Erasmo Wagner looks into the hopper and thinks there isn't space in the world for so much trash. Shall everyone be suffocated by it? A sea of squalor to sacrifice humanity in its own waste.

"There's too much trash in the world . . . maybe that's it," Erasmo Wagner murmurs under his breath.

"Does it bother you?" Valtair asks.

"Not in the least. I know there'll always be work."

"And they talk about an ecosystem, right?"

"I don't give a crap about any fucking ecosystem. When the world's deep in its own shit, I'll be long gone." He hesitates. Lights a cigarette. "Don't give me that look. You don't give a crap either. What really bothers me is my bad tooth. Both. They hurt like fuck."

He squeezes his face and shudders. He spits blood into the hopper.

"That tooth decay will outlast you," says Valtair. "A tooth will last millions of years. Even a rotten tooth."

Erasmo Wagner says nothing else. He's mute for the rest of the trip to the dump. He's wiped out. It was a shitty day and he hopes the night improves, although it's suffocating.

CHAPTER 2

He switched off the jackhammer late in the afternoon; it was raining hard. Work's hampered by rain. Alandelon's been breaking asphalt for six years. His body is cut and rigid, like his brain: brutish. He's Erasmo Wagner's youngest brother; Edivardes, who works the sewers, is his cousin. He hasn't broken half the asphalt his brother has. He'll have to break another fifteen kilometers of asphalt to catch up. It's heavy work.

As he goes to sit down, he sheds the long-sleeved yellow coveralls, the helmet, and helps himself to a bottle of water. His heart's racing. It's always like this when he finishes work. His body vibrates long after he's set down the jackhammer. His muscles tense and his body is desensitized; stick him, puncture him, and he won't notice. High-tension electric currents run in his veins, muscles, and bones. After that, there's silence.

He's deaf for hours after work, so he compensates by talking loudly. He needs to find another job before he becomes permanently deaf. But if everyone worried, who'd be left to tear up asphalt? He gets it: jobs like these lead directly to heaven. It's a hell too hot for the devil. There's early retirement. Most workers are scarred.

In the rearview of the pickup truck on the way back to the construction company, he coifs his beard. He takes pride in his beard. He trims it regularly and combs it carefully. He looks at it for long stretches without knowing what to think. When a man breaks asphalt, collects trash, or unclogs sewers daily, his brain becomes undernourished, unable to grasp more details. Unless it's truly captured by something, focus is difficult.

Erasmo Wagner is already home when he arrives. They live together. They take care of a house, a yard, and two domestic milking goats: Divina and Rosa Flor. They milk them daily. Sell some and consume the rest. It's not much, but they've learned to live on little.

"Tomorrow, Mr. Aparício will bring his goat," says Alandelon.

"But I haven't decided if I want to breed them," Erasmo Wagner responds.

"His goat's registered, and award-winning."

Erasmo Wagner grabs another piece of toast from the plate on the table and dips it into the soft yolk of his fried egg. He takes a sip of fresh coffee, before putting the egg-toast in his mouth. Alandelon lights a cigarette and leans on the kitchen door. The constant droning in his ears—like the motor of a water pump—deafens him. It'll be some time before it clears. Erasmo Wagner continues to talk and Alandelon follows the crux of the conversation with few audible words.

"And what if they really go on strike?" Alandelon asks

"We're required to go along. If the truck drivers stop, we stop."

Erasmo Wagner is nostalgic and sighs. The reality of his job is pretty despicable. High-risk compensation is negligible. Guys like him risk their lives to hang onto a job. Sometimes a pal falls off a truck, is run over, catches a contagious disease, loses an arm or a hand in the crusher, gets a hernia from carrying too much weight, becomes an invalid, has to retire, and is cast aside like the trash he's collected on the sidewalks and dumped in the landfills. His color, smell, and taste don't matter. What he thinks, desires, plans, and feels doesn't matter. What matters is that the trash is picked up, taken far away, and made to disappear, along with him.

"If they don't want to pay what the union's demanding, there'll be no pickup."

The whirring of the water pump motor in Alandelon's ears

diminishes. It's a relief when this happens. He takes analgesics every eight hours to deal with the buzzing and the headaches that threaten his emotional stability. Yes, Alandelon's a stable character.

"Erasmo, do you think they really mean it?"

"I'm sure of it. You'll see, Alandelon, you'll see the city rot."

Erasmo Wagner washes his hands in a grimy sink at the back of the yard. He just woke and it's still very early, but he anticipates it'll be a scorcher in a few hours. He greets the goats. They ruminate. He picks up a black tin pail and a wooden stool, and he takes a seat next to Divina, the plumpest. She's agitated. She stomps in the dirt. He needs to tie her up. Divina was always frisky, a pesky she-goat.

He grabs hold of a teat and pulls. Milk jets into the black bucket. Erasmo Wagner spies the pail's contents, and then carefully inspects it. He's not satisfied.

"Erasmo, isn't there any bread?" Alandelon yells. He's standing next to Erasmo Wagner.

"Go buy some," his brother yells back.

"Bakery isn't open, you know?"

Erasmo regrets the probable lack of breakfast. But, he's working the night shift. So it's no skin off his back. He worries about Alandelon's deafness. He's too young to be so scarred. For his brother to hear him, he has to yell, and this makes his throat hurt.

"Why?" yells Erasmo Wagner.

"Someone killed the baker," yells Alandelon. "There's a note on the door says he was murdered this morning."

"So go to the other one. On the lower street."

"It's too far. I'd be late for work. I'm going to eat yesterday's toast, okay?"

Alandelon is holding a plate with toast on it. He's standing next to his brother but, even so, every word is yelled.

What can we do? sighs Erasmo Wagner.

"Go ahead. I'll find something later."

As he says this, he returns his attention to the pail. He milks Divina a little more, hot jets hit the pail, and he confirms the watery milk is lumpy, pus-filled, and yellowish. She's got mastitis. He throws the contaminated milk at the foot of a banana tree. He'll need to vaccinate the goat.

A sick Divina is something to worry about. She gives on average four liters of milk per day; approximately, 120 liters per month. He gets two reais for each liter. He's looking at a loss of 240 reais per month. And the roof needs repairs. The money the goat earns goes into a clay piggybank. There'll be no savings this month. He'll deal with the bad tooth for a few more weeks. And the roof may cave during the next rainstorm.

He gets the other goat, Rosa Flor. She's a sweetheart with honey-colored eyes. Her first jets of frothy, perfumed milk inside the pail suggest health. He milks Rosa Flor under the eyes of Divina, who ruminates loudly. She's furious. He finds it's prudent to keep her tied to the wooden post until he's done.

"You milked Divina without washing your hands, didn't you?"

Alandelon is at the kitchen table. He doesn't respond. He just eats his toast and drinks his coffee.

"You milked Divina without washing your hands!" yells Erasmo Wagner.

"Did you say something?"

"Of course I said something. I've been saying something for some time."

Alandelon seems to agree, and takes another sip of coffee. Erasmo Wagner waits for his brother to respond.

"What did you say?" yells Alandelon.

"Did you milk Divina without washing your hands?"

"Did I?"

"Did—You—Milk—Her?"

"When?"

"I don't know . . . Did you ever milk her with dirty hands?"

He thinks on it. Chews on a bite of toast and responds:

"I don't remember. Why?"

"She's sick. Her milk's sour."

"What?"

"She's sick. Mastitis. Now I need to buy her a vaccine."

"What?"

"If you say 'What?' one more time, I'll punch you in the nose."

Alandelon hardly hears a thing his brother says, but he knows he's angry. He yanks tufts of hair from his beard when he's very irritated. So, Alandelon swallows a last mouthful of toast, grabs his knapsack, and hurries off to work. Erasmo Wagner gets a telephone card and walks the two blocks to the nearest public phone.

"She's got sour milk."

"Is there pus?"

"Yes."

"You need to vaccinate. It'll cost you eighty-five reais."

"Is there a cheaper one?"

"No. That's it."

Erasmo Wagner pulls strands from his crisp beard. There's no alternative. He needs to take care of his personal investments. He wants to breed his goats.

"Bring the vaccine in the afternoon," he says to the man on the phone.

"No, can't go there. Bring her here at night, and I'll do something for her."

"I work tonight. I'll bring her tomorrow."

There's nothing to be done but to do it. He rushes home and finds Mr. Aparício and his billy goat, Tonhão, waiting at his gate.

"Hey there, Erasmo, I brought Tonhão to put with your goats."

"I hadn't made up my mind yet."

"But, man, you've got to breed them. Tonhão's a prize buck. The only prized buck in the region. He'll service them good.

Keep him for a few days and then I'll come get my boy. He's the best!"

A van approaches, and Mr. Aparício says goodbye:

"Yes, son . . . I have to go. Take good care of my Tonhão, you hear?"

He jumps into the van and leaves Erasmo Wagner and Tonhão parked on the sidewalk. Before the van screeches away blinding Erasmo Wagner with dust, he notices a golden charm hanging from Tonhão's neck. The animal swaggers. After a bleat, the charm sways on his neck. The day begins with difficulties, and by the look on this goat's face, it's only going to get worse.

***

Before he was a city trash collector, Erasmo Wagner picked up temporary work on trucks that dumped trash in the landfill. He spent months on the odd job. Anything to survive hard times. And that's when he contemplated the horror and misery. Organic and human trash. Society's byproduct.

When they approached the area to dump a load, they would be surrounded by people waiting anxiously for the detritus of others. A day's detritus. And it was always a party.

Every day brought a rare state of joy. A fulminating impact of the horror. Many who survive on trash also live in trash. They camp around a lake of decomposition known as the landfill leachate.

First time he heard the expression, he was saddened. The truck driver said: "It'll disturb you. After years unloading in that spot, I still dream about that lake."

An unbearably stinky liquid pollutant made from the biological, chemical, and physical decomposition of organic residues in trash. This liquid creates ditches between the dunes of detritus, scoring the earth until it empties in a unified hole that forms an immense lake.

It's not the fiery lake of burning sulfur of Hell. It's worse. All things end in leachate. Leftovers, toxic residues, and unburied stiffs find their end there. Erasmo Wagner's cousin was assassinated and dumped at that same landfill. A mortal error. When he nears the lake, he mutters a prayer. Leachate is an interminable and damned lament; spoiled tears from flagellated eyes.

Erasmo Wagner loves working the nightshift. The city's quiet, the garbage piled high on sidewalks in front of buildings. Even in hot weather, there's an evening breeze.

No rushing. His steps echo. His loud jokes echo too. On the nightshift, there's Valtair, the rookie, and he can count on Jeremias, another trash collector, to be there too.

He hasn't got a left hand. It was shredded in the cane juicer at a bar where he worked. Maybe it's why he's so handy. He compensates for his disability by doing the work of two men, and so demonstrates his worthiness. With the help of his left stub, he hoists a large bag, and sets his eyes on the truck's compacter, which has moved farther down the road.

"You forgot this one," says Jeremias to Valtair. "Be cleaner, guy. You pick up the trash but let half of it fall into the street. To work trash you got to be tidy, get it?"

Jeremais likes order and cleanliness. The quality of his service is apparent on any street. He doesn't leave a cigarette butt behind. He doesn't make a mess; he leaves no trail. Like many garbage men, Jeremias doesn't leave a footprint where he goes. He's a clean man and he smells of lavender. Even when he sweats.

"I've got a billy goat at home," says Erasmo Wagner.

"Billy-o problems? I've got those too," says Valtair.

"No, a real billy goat. His name's Tonhão. He's to breed with my milking goats. Only can you trust a goat? No."

"Goats stink. They shit all the time," says Valtair.

Erasmo Wagner jumps onto the back of the truck and balances on the tailgate; Jeremias and Valtair follow. The tailgate is slippery. It's necessary to hold on as the truck suddenly starts and stops, or risk falling off. They continue on to the next street.

"Divina, my plumpest, produces the most, but she's got sour milk. I need to give her a shot," he scratches his beard. "My tooth's rotted, her milk's rotted . . ."

"You're cursed," says Jeremias.

They jump off the truck at the next collection spot. Jeremias puts a rubber band around his transistor radio and raises it over his head. He secures the little radio to his left ear, passes the rubber band across his forehead, and wraps it around his head. He likes to listen to music while he works. The others think he looks hilarious, but he doesn't care. He fidgets with the antenna, finds a station, and sings along.

Erasmo Wagner pokes his tooth. It hurts. He puts on gloves and runs to pick up bags. The truck's always noisy and echoes the length of the street. Valtair's a klutz, and leaves half the trash wherever he passes and has to run back to get it. Jeremias concentrates on making efficient moves and on the music from his transistor radio. It's like any other night. But Erasmo Wagner's distressed. He's had this feeling before, when he was incarcerated. It tends to come before a tragedy. In jail, black clouds foretold bad luck. It's what he feels now.

At the end of the street, he sees a youth drop a huge black trash bag by a tree on the sidewalk, and quickly walk away. Erasmo Wagner sees black clouds. His heart beats faster. This is a bad sign. He begins to put some distance between himself and his fellow workers. The guy who left the bag hasn't turned the corner yet. Erasmo Wagner quickens his pace in the direction of the bag on the ground. He knows the contents of some bags by their smell, shape, and solidness.

With a pocketknife, he tears open the bag. The boy inside inhales the night breeze sharply. His chest is cut open and crudely sewn shut with black nylon thread. He's purple all over. And looking at the contents of the bag, at the garbage this boy has become, Erasmo Wagner can tell organs are missing. He's hollow inside. He dies with open eyes, unable to utter a word.

"Erasmo!" yells Valtair. "Whatcha doin' there, man? Garbage's over here."

"They left a bag here," Erasmo Wagner yells back.

Valtair runs toward Erasmo Wagner, pounding his chest to defend himself.

"I collected all of it. Don't blame me," says Valtair, approaching. "I picked up all the fucking trash and didn't leave any behind."

"But someone did," says Erasmo Wagner.

Valtair sees the dead boy in the bag. He stifles a desire to vomit. The garbage only stopped disturbing his senses recently, but he's not prepared to see cadavers on the sidewalk.

Erasmo Wagner sets to run after the guy who abandoned the bag, and disappears around the corner. He searches night's breaches and the city's nooks, but doesn't find anyone. He remembers hearing a car ignition. The guy was faster than him.

He returns to the body of the boy in the black garbage bag. Valtair's on his knees and prays.

"Get up. We need to notify the police."

"Who would do something like this, Erasmo?"

"I don't know, Valtair. I really don't know."

Erasmo Wagner crouches down and tries to close the plastic bag to protect its contents. The truck driver gets the police in gear. Jeremias, the one-handed man, spies the contents of the bag and says:

"We need to go. There's a lot of trash to collect tonight."

"But he's dead," says Valtair.

"Right. He doesn't need us. The trash does."

Saying this, Jeremias turns up the volume on the transistor radio and goes back to collecting trash. Erasmo Wagner holds on to Valtair's arm and walks beside him.

"He was so young, Erasmo, just a boy."

The city gets to everyone: boys, women, orphans, old folks. The city makes no exceptions. Everything becomes trash. Leftovers, an old mattress, a broken refrigerator, or a dead boy.

Anything scandalous the city covers over and seals off. They collect what's wretched and dispose of it at the filthy, faraway margins.

CHAPTER 3

Edivardes unclogs toilets, sinks, traps, cisterns, pipes, drain vents, waste lines. He wallows in the filth more than pigs. Working in the filth produced by others he manages to survive in a dignified manner. He has two daughters who study in private schools. And to give himself this luxury, he also cleans septic tanks, leach fields, consolidation ponds, wastewater treatment systems, and grease and chemical product disposals.

"You mean to say the goats are sick?" asks Edivardes.

"Not all of them, just Divina. She needs a vaccine. She's got milk stasis," replies Erasmo Wagner.

"So her milk's sour."

"That's right."

Erasmo Wagner and his cousin, Edivardes, are having breakfast at a bakery while they wait for Alandelon. They meet there on Saturday mornings. When Erasmo Wagner and Alandelon were orphaned, Edivardes's mother raised them. An aunt is more than mother and father. An aunt is the person beneath God. Being just beneath God, she's susceptible to every ill and malice. And God's hand rests on her, since she's sick with a degenerative disease. She's wilting. Her wrinkled dark skin has the texture of fried pigskin. It's possible to count her remaining hairs and teeth. She can't walk. Lucidity is preserved for her in stories of the past. Every day, Erasmo Wagner visits her, listens to her stories, and reads to her from a section of the Old Testament.

Edivardes drips a little milk into his coffee and Erasmo Wagner takes his black, no sugar.

"Do you remember Manolo Amanso who raised goats on Rua 35?"

"I know he had Brucellosis," replies Erasmo Wagner.

"That's right," Edivardes affirms. "Damned goats."

Erasmo Wagner lights a cigarette. Edivardes clears his throat. Alandelon enters the bakery. Edivardes calls his name. He walks past and goes into the bathroom without seeing them.

"What's with him, Erasmo?"

"He's not hearing well."

"The jackhammer's killing him."

Erasmo Wagner draws on his cigarette and taps his fingers on the table.

"They say the sickness was passed on to Mr. Amanso by a sick goat. It had sores on its skin," comments Erasmo Wagner.

"No one knows how long he carried it. Could've been years. In the end, it reached his kidneys, heart, liver. There was little left of him," concluded Edivardes.

Alandelon pulls up a chair and sits next to his kin. He looks preoccupied. He orders. He wants coffee with milk, toast, and scrambled eggs. Alandelon's booming voice doesn't startle the waiter. He's used to it. Every Saturday is the same. The same order. The same unhinged voice.

"By the looks of him, something's happened," says Erasmo Wagner.

"Huh?"

"WHAT HAPPENED?"

Alandelon runs his hand through his soft beard. It's clean and perfumed. He looks away to a mildew stain on the wall in front of him. A thin stain that runs into a muddy and foul river and opens out everywhere. He returns his attention to his brother.

"The goat ate your shoe."

Erasmo Wagner takes a sip of coffee. This gesture, unaccompanied by a single word, means: "Continue, I'm listening."

"Your black dress shoe."

Erasmo Wagner pulls hairs from his beard. Alandelon sees it, and knows he must tell everything.

"The goat dragged your pants from the line and through the yard, then peed on them. Erasmo, there wasn't time to stop him. When I saw it, it was already too late. I slapped the goat. But it ran the fence. And so, also broke the fence, and now it's fucking the neighbor's bitch."

Edivardes looks apologetic and blows his nose with a blue kerchief. Erasmo Wagner stops pulling his beard and has a sip of his black coffee. He appreciates Saturday mornings. It's when he feels most respected. The dirty work as a garbage man pays for a wholesome and honest breakfast once a week. Many don't have this privilege. Many have kids to raise. Wives to keep. Like a beast of burden, Erasmo Wagner is sterile, and like that beast, he lives to carry loads. Erasmo Wagner will never have any progeny. He won't self-perpetuate. He shall end in himself and it gives him an agreeable pleasure to know he'll leave no trace.

"I'm going to finish my coffee. I'm going to read the sports section. Then I'm going to get up, sharpen my knife, and kill that bloody goat. I'll dice it. I'll cook it in its own blood. I'll make sausage with its tripe and prepare a *Sarrabulho* stew with its nuts."

"But Mr. Aparício will want to know what happened to his goat," comments Edivardes.

"The goat's in my yard. In my yard, I'm the law. I get to kill that goat and anything else I want."

"Right. You're right. It'll be more lucrative dead," quips Edivardes.

"Not to mention it's done nothing with my goats. And has only caused damage."

Alandelon, distracted and deaf, says:

"Did someone say *Sarrabulho*?"

***

Alandelon is kneeling in the corner of the yard sharpening a yellow-handled knife. He remains like this for some time. The sky is cloudy and he feels the pressure of swollen clouds settling down. The morning resembles late afternoon. This upsets him. The roof of his house needs urgent repairs. It won't stand up to another downpour.

On the other side of the barbed wire, separating his yard from his neighbor's, Tonhão, the buck, runs back and forth, bleating, swinging the little gold charm around its neck. Edivardes looks on with crossed arms. He doesn't like to run. He feels tired. His talent lies in making concentrated effort.

Erasmo Wagner walks with such a heavy step that he leaves footprints in the muddy yard. The buck runs behind the bitch; brave dog. It bares teeth to Erasmo Wagner. Threatens to advance. Tonhão, the coward, remains lofty, protectively escorted by the bitch. Erasmo Wagner jumps the goat, and the bitch jumps Erasmo Wagner. It's got his left hand in its mouth. He punches the dog; it doesn't let go of his hand. He twists from side to side as its teeth pierce his flesh. Still, it doesn't let go. He throws it against a wall; Tonhão butts him in the legs. He kicks the buck. He holds the bitch against the wall until it trembles and faints.

His hand's bleeding. An impressively truculent dog's tooth has passed through his flesh and is anchored in his bone. Dark old dog. He's in a lot of pain. He advances upon Tonhão and punches the goat between its eyes. The prize goat stops strutting, and falls over to the right. Erasmo Wagner drags it by the horns back into his yard. He ties a rope around its neck, tethers the rope to a tree, and gags it. This way it can't bite when it's conscious again.

"Isn't it better to put it out of its misery now?" asks Edivardes.

"I wouldn't be capable of killing an animal while it sleeps," replies Erasmo Wagner.

He swallows the blood seeping from his rotten, aching tooth. "I like to look it in the eye. So it knows why it's dying."

***

Erasmo Wagner lives in the place where he was born. He's moved three times, but always within the same neighborhood. When Alandelon was very little, old Mendes, the neighborhood tycoon, killed his parents. He owned the only newspaper stand, a truck stop diner five-kilometers out, some market stalls, and a gas station. Erasmo Wagner's parents worked for the old man. His mother cooked in the diner and his father stacked gas cylinders at the gas station.

Old Mendes had a long gray beard. He liked kids. Every year he dressed up as Santa Claus and gave out bags of candy in honor of Saints Cosmas and Damian. He abused kids with the same devotion, tears in his eyes. Alandelon was very young. He ate peanut brittle while the old man sucked him behind a stack of old gas containers in his yard.

His parents arrived as he licked his lips in satisfaction. Alandelon loves peanut brittle. He doesn't remember a thing. His father threatened to go to the police; old Mendes threatened to kill them, and carried out his threat.

When Erasmo Wagner was old enough and strong enough, he thrust a paring of pointed iron through the old man's neck. Old Mendes was groggy and went to open the front door for the boy who delivered milk, bread, orange cake, and Melba toast from the bakery. He managed to take two steps back, before falling on his knees with the rusty splinter in his throat. While he was dying, Erasmo Wagner stared deeply into his eyes. And he saw that the old man understood the reason for his death.

He was arrested; he let his beard grow and served his time. Erasmo Wagner is considered a cretin. Brutish. Soulless. And, also bearded.

A bearded cretin for most people. A martyr for those who know his story.

In prison, he taught himself to be attentive to imminent fatality. His senses sharpened and his skill saved him from death twice. Erasmo Wagner never feels sad or alone. He doesn't know what it means to suffer for love. He doesn't search for meaning in life. His thoughts are clear and objective. He does his work and survives. He intends to buy a used car and go on a road trip. He'd like to die on the highway. He wants to finish out his days roaming the Earth, and leave no trace.

His profession teaches that the trash collected on city sidewalks piles up elsewhere. The trash leaves tracks. No one's ever free of remains and leftovers. Sometimes at the landfill, he smokes two or three cigarettes while he contemplates the vestiges of a city, what's left behind by citizens whose paths he crossed hours earlier. Erasmo Wagner will find a way to take his tracks with him on the day he ceases to exist, but he's not sure how he'll do it.

CHAPTER 4

Tonhão drags his muzzle along the ground, trying to remove the gag. He bucks to rid himself of the rope around his neck. His charm clangs. Rosa Flor, the youngest, is restless. Divina, with an inflamed udder full of sour milk, looks on apathetically. She's taken the vaccine and everything suggests that Erasmo Wagner's investment of eighty-five reais was for naught. The two are tied to a fence. Tonhão's presence disturbs their senses.

Edivardes alerts him that the goat's awake. The sharpened knife waits on the edge of the sink for the cut. Alandelon's on the roof patching and splicing before the rain. He lines the roof with aluminum sheets.

Erasmo Wagner finishes his cigarette, walks to the sink, washes his hands, and picks up the knife. Tonhão is more agitated. Edivardes observes Erasmo Wagner ungag the animal, who rubs its horns on the tree. It baaed and uttered a tremulous bleat. It capers to escape the cord. Erasmo Wagner holds the goat by the horns. Looks into its eyes. Remembers old Mendes. And stops. He can't go on. He returns to the sink, washes his face and refreshes himself, and seeks courage. That's why he takes cold baths, to stiffen his courage.

Standing before Tonhão again, he looks in the goat's eyes and there's old Mendes again. Erasmo Wagner leans against the tree and lets his body go limp. He thought that story was over: having done his time, having sacrificed years of his life to repair the harm he'd done.

Having stuck the old man with a jagged shard of iron seemed

fair to him in his own view of justice, but there was something more. Something that wafted in on the hircus odor of a prize buck.

"What is it?" says Edivardes, approaching.

"I can't kill this goat," says Erasmo Wagner, panting.

"What's with you?"

"Don't know."

Edivardes takes the knife from Erasmo Wagner's hand and grabs Tonhão by the horns. The buck defends itself. It emits a low groan and then some grunts. The malodor exhaled by the animal is acrid and fetid. Since it's not castrated. Tonhão exhales a putrid odor whenever anxious. Edivardes holds the knife in midair. He reconsiders. On his face, a wrinkle appears from his effort to understand.

"Did it say my name?"

"How so?" asks Erasmo Wagner.

"I heard this buck say my name."

"I only heard a bleat."

"But I heard it when it said E-di-var-des."

Tonhão rubs its horns in the ground. It digs in with a right cleat.

Alandelon comes down off the roof and walks toward the back of the yard. He's drawn to the commotion of the goat slaughter.

"How do you mean it said your name?" asks Alandelon. "It's a goat."

Alandelon picks the knife up off the ground; he holds the swaggering caprine by the horns. He wipes the muddy backyard knife on his pants. He shakes his head. He's never seen two men who couldn't kill a goat. But he's used to perforating asphalt, tearing up roadways, sloughing up highways. For him, slitting a goat's throat is a simple action. Watched by his cousin and his brother, he bucks up. He's never done anything these two couldn't do.

He bends forward, searches for the ideal spot for a blow;

hopes it'll take just one. And then he falls over to the side, as if struck by the sleeve of a sword at the back of his neck, and then there's a clap of thunder. Alandelon's body convulses and he loses consciousness.

Tonhão digs into the earth, scrapes its horns on the ground, and makes the charm chime. The goat sees Alandelon's outstretched body rapidly soaked by heavy rain.

Perplexed, Erasmo Wagner wipes the excess precipitation off his face, grabs the muddy knife and, with a single stroke, cuts the cord that ties Tonhão to the tree. The freed goat runs for protection from the rain beneath an old, forgotten table at the back of the yard.

Edivardes is dragging Alandelon toward the house, and now Erasmo Wagner grabs his feet and, thus, they carry him and place him inert upon the sofa.

***

Edivardes sits on an armchair next to the sofa where Alandelon's resting. They're silent. Erasmo Wagner settles into his seat and rests his elbows on the table. They're afraid to say anything. Edivardes turns on the radio. Erasmo Wagner lights a cigarette. Alandelon turns over onto his side and snorts. They listen to radio static and falling rain. It's as if, for a few minutes, the world collapsed in silence and carried Erasmo Wagner's thoughts down with it.

Edivardes worries about something he hears on the radio. He gets up to tune it better. He adjusts the antenna, and discovers the only way to stop the static is by holding the tip. Erasmo Wagner returns to the surface of his thoughts. Sanitation workers have gone on strike. Drivers stopped an hour ago. Trash collectors followed. It's common to stop at midnight, but it's noon. They drove the trucks back to the yard and went home.

Trash collection and street sweeping have come to a standstill.

Workers pledge themselves to the struggle until the end. They've got to see it through, if they cave, in a few hours or days, they won't be as effective as they hope to be. They want to accomplish what they've not had the courage to achieve before. They demand better working conditions. They need medical assistance. They need sunblock: skin cancer's on the rise. They need places to sit in the truck, last week three trash collectors fell off dilapidated tailgates: one was crushed to death, another will be paralyzed, and the luckiest has a fractured femur and pelvis.

People wish they'd return to work immediately; wish to be free of their refuse and leftovers. They want their trash collected and taken far away. For a miserable wage. In deplorable conditions. They don't know the disease, the risk, and neglect a sanitation worker confronts.

They decide to let the city rot. Everyone will have to deal with their own shit. They'll have to cover their own tracks. The government's inflexible with regard to a wage increase, and sanitation workers' convictions are immutable. They'll let pests and pestilence take over every corner of the city. Let the state pick up its own trash! Let citizens get rid of their own detritus.

"The city will rot," says Erasmo Wagner.

"Think it'll last long?" asks Edivardes.

"Seems so. Folks are tired of the wretched conditions at work."

"Aren't we all," says Edivardes, and he begins to cut his nails with the clippers on his keychain.

Erasmo Wagner turns off the radio. The static's bothering him.

"They're serving *Sarrabulho* at Cristóvão's bar today. Take the goat to him," says Edivardes. "He'll put its intestines in the stew. He'll appreciate the flavor of the goat's kidney."

"Leave the animal quiet, for now."

"What do you intend to do?"

"I haven't decided, so leave it alone," says Erasmo Wagner.

Alandelon turns over and falls off the sofa. This wakes him. He groans. Scratches his balls. Without a word, he gets up and goes to the bathroom.

"Suppose he's okay?" asks Edivardes.

"Seems like it."

Erasmo Wagner walks to the window that looks out over the yard. The buck is lying under an old table, napping. The rain is intense, but the lightning and thunder have stopped. Guilty silence.

The milk goats are strangely quiet. Divina's apathetic, yet she's normally agitated on rainy days; she gets prickly and likes to make noise. After her vaccine, she hasn't been the same. She refuses to eat.

From the bathroom they hear the toilet flush, and a dry cough. Alandelon comes to the room asking what happened. Edivardes tells the whole story of trying to kill the goat.

"I think it's best to leave Tonhão alive," says Alandelon. "I don't like the animal much."

"There's something about that goat," finishes Erasmo Wagner.

Alandelon turns up the television to high volume and finds a news channel. Seconds later, he yells, in his way:

"Erasmo, you on strike?"

"Mark my words, Alandelon. The city will rot."

***

The light through the window is low because of the hour. Cristóvão, a Portuguese of few words, cuts two pairs of cow kidneys into cubes on a wooden cutting board over the sink. He shoos flies that insistently circle the thick, well-cured pork short ribs and loin. The bone belongs to the animal's spine or vertebra. Cristóvão sun-cured the bone himself. It's just right. He dries his hands on the dish towel hanging over his left shoulder, walks to the door of the small kitchen, and switches the light on. He returns to the sink. He doesn't like his kitchen staff to prepare the *Sarrabulho*. Instead he uses the time to remember his native land: Ponte de Lima. His mother specialized in this dish and helped spread a taste for it throughout northern Portugal. He's proud of this fact. He'll take this family tradition to the grave with him. None of his children can stand the smell of *Sarrabulho*. They can't condone this much blood in any meal.

In other basins on the sink, he's set aside pork throats and hearts, cow's liver, blood-sausage and pig's lung, and a little chicken fat. In a medium bowl, he's put minced tomatoes, peppers, onions, and added the garlic, bay leaf, and green and black olives. He'll sauté it all in lard, because Cristóvão doesn't use soybean oil. He was raised on pork: lard, blood, bones, and offal. With so much pork in him, he feels part pig. He prepares the food with deep respect for the swine and for himself.

Having diced the kidneys, he checks the time and keeps an eye on the lard in the big pot on the stove. He figures it's hot enough to braise the meats, and begins to throw them in. Customers are arriving. The smell of *Sarrabulho* escapes into the bar and out onto the street. Dogs circle near the establishment, but they'll have to wait for leftovers.

Edivardes sits at a table with Erasmo Wagner and Alandelon. They discuss the sanitation strike that started a short time ago. Erasmo Wagner's on the side of the masses. Whether it goes on for days or ends within hours, it doesn't matter. He doesn't think it'll make any difference. He expects little from life. All he wants is to relish a good, meaty *Sarrabulho*.

Edivardes complains about his mother's illness. She's feeling more pain, and she sleeps less, worrying so about her degenerative condition. Erasmo Wagner would like to do more for his aunt. He knows there's no relief for her pain, she's suffering from an incurable illness that will take her to the grave. He feels impotent to do anything that could generate any real change in his aunt's life. When he holds her frail hand, he wants to cry. His bedridden aunt chews on her tongue and moans from her lungs.

Once, Erasmo Wagner found a woman near death in a

dumpster. She was just like a strip of beef jerky. Dark, dried, salted meat. Human remnants were mixed with organic trash, Tetra Pak packaging, and cans of peas. But despite all the filth in this world, he knows too that he, Alandelon, and Edivardes, will provide a decent burial for his aunt, including a crown of magnolias, her favorites.

The odor of *Sarrabulho* overtakes the bar. It envelops tables, chairs, counter, and pool table. The smell of coagulated pig's blood inspires the imagination and whets the appetite.

Erasmo Wagner stretches his neck, drums his fingers on the table, and gets up to go to the bathroom in silence. On his way, he spots Cristóvão making the *Sarrabulho*. For him, the smell is a fragrant perfume. The *Sarrabulho* smells so good and the taste is splendid, compared to the sour and rotten smell of trash that he's used to.

In the bathroom, while he pees, he reads a sentence inscribed above the urinal that softens his heart: SUZETE LOVES ERASMO WAGNER. The naughty girl said she'd do this for him. Let every man at that bar know it while they piss, Erasmo Wagner has a girl who truly loves him. He takes it as a gesture of love, with a musty dose of perversion, immersed in the sour smell of piss left by dozens of men who've been there. He leaves the restroom and returns to the table.

"Erasmo, I think I've got a job for you," says Edivardes. "So long as the strike continues, you could be my helper. The guy who's with me is a terrible worker. I let him go. I'm looking to replace him, and you could fill in."

Erasmo Wagner holds a Band-Aid in his left hand, the one bitten by the dog. He's bleeding.

"Sure. That could work," he says, getting up to go to the bathroom again.

He puts his wound under running water. Squeezes, hard, the hole that the tooth left. Spits blood. The blood is from his rotting tooth. Erasmo Wagner bleeds from two holes. As if he were slowly bleeding out. He covers the wound with the

Band-Aid, and sticks his finger in his mouth against the loose molar. He gently wiggles the tooth. His pain gradually increases and that's how he anesthetizes the area. He takes his finger out of his mouth. Spits in the sink. Swallows water from the faucet. Washes his face and finds his moxie. He places two fingers in his mouth, and with a low groan pulls out the rotten molar. The blackened tooth reeks. He stuffs a wad of toilet paper in its place to stop the gushing blood. He returns to the table. His beer is warm. His mouth is full of toilet paper. He takes the wad out of his mouth. It's soaked in blood. He drains his beer, sloshes it around, and swallows.

"That tooth was killing me." He takes the tooth out of his pocket. "Look. I'm saving this misery. Evil tooth."

Nanico, the waiter, brings a tray of *Sarrabulho* to the table. The three men say grace and serve themselves. The amount of blood in this dish has it resembling a kind of sacrifice of atonement for their sins. The waiter goes to the door to shoo away the dogs that are howling because of the odor. They don't understand their turn will come; these remains and leftovers are for them. But dogs are impatient; and when starved, they act as anyone would—even you and me.

CHAPTER 5

Days have passed. Some dirtier and more sour than others. Hot days, the kinds of days that make the sun crackle. Black clouds form. Vultures gather: the skies belong to them. And from above, in groups, they take siege of the city. Airports are alerted to the imminent danger of colliding with a vulture during take-off and landing; the high probability of falling out of the sky if a vulture's pulled into a plane's turbine.

On the asphalt, trash piles up, especially on public squares, street corners, and sidewalks. Some streets are blocked by trash. It completely blankets the asphalt. Rats reproduce abundantly and attack people in broad daylight. Hospitals are full to capacity. Cases of infectious disease erupt daily. Part of the electrical system is down, gnawed through by rodents on some streets. They starve. Even amid all that garbage, even with so much rotting food, they can't satiate their appetites. Rats want chaos. And the authorities still won't consider a salary readjustment for the working class. Nevertheless, the working class holds out.

Private trash collectors try to contain the chaos at schools, hospitals, and penitentiaries. Even so, it's too much trash. Some schools suspend classes. Hospital debris isn't always picked up. Patients and waste pile up: along with used needles, broken glass, breadcrumbs, and porridge.

The orange Transporter rattles along the pothole-riddled street with no memory of the asphalt laid down six years ago. The dust rising doesn't reach the black smoke coming from the muffler. Edivardes stops the van in front of the house where he lives with Erasmo Wagner, who's crouching in the back yard. He's just buried his goat, Divina, it's not been an hour. The animal convulsed for two days. He's confident he did everything he could to save her. Two nights in a row, he dozed off while massaging her head in her pen. He prayed. He believed she'd improve. But morning found her dead with her eyes wide open.

Before breakfast, Erasmo Wagner gets a shovel, digs a deep hole, and buries Divina. He puts a stone on her grave and says a prayer.

Tonhão wanders the yard, despondent. While saying his prayer, Erasmo Wagner senses a vague rumbling from the animal. But his desire to raise goats has been buried there under that stone, in that small tomb.

He'd negotiated a good price for Rosa Flor. He wanted to complete the sale before she got sick too. He managed 150 reais for Rosa Flor's sweet-smelling milk and tender meat. She's sold live. The money will be useful now since his other bad tooth has become a poisonous thorn in his mouth.

Another sip of coffee and he goes to take a bath. He's dirty with earth and goat odors. Goat permeates even his thoughts.

Edivardes turns on the TV and sits on the sofa. Alandelon eats his breakfast in the kitchen. His hearty chewing can be heard in the living room. He'll need to be at the contractor's in a few hours. Next week he's working a highway construction. It's the first he'll help to build. It'll take months. There'll be little rest and his body has to be fit to operate the jackhammer for long hours.

After a while tearing up asphalt, he feels life pulling him down. He has the habit of opening small holes in the yard, digging into food, sinking his fingers into cakes, and pulling the soft center out of bread. Alandelon likes to dig. He remembers liking it ever since he was a kid. He also excavates when he looks at a person. His eyes are hole diggers; no sooner does he see a person than he begins to bore. Most people want to move ahead, want to climb in life. He wants to tunnel down, dig a trench, since he has the impression that in a subterranean fissure, he'll find something that belongs to him, but he doesn't know what exactly.

Erasmo Wagner exits the bathroom dressed for work, a lit cigarette between his lips. He grabs his knapsack from the bedroom, and the three head to the van. Edivardes opens the door and discovers Tonhão inside, seated on the newspaper that lines the floor. He questions Tonhão's presence there; the door was closed.

"I think he wants to come with us," says Alandelon.

"How come? He's a goat. I'm not taking a goat for a joyride. Maybe a dog. But can we just agree the door was closed?" Edivardes responds.

Edivardes pulls Tonhão by the cord. The goat doesn't budge. He tries forcing him, but the animal weighs a ton. Not one of them is able to move it from its place. So, they agree to take Tonhão with them. Erasmo Wagner puts Rosa Flor in the back seat next to Tonhão, since he has to turn the milk goat over to its new owner. The buck looks at the doeling and lowers its head to the van floor. Tonhão only likes bitches.

"This goat's dumb," says Erasmo Wagner, flicking the butt of his cigarette onto the street, before climbing into the van.

***

As they drive, they see the extent of the horror caused by the sanitation strike. In the deserted, seemingly rural area where they live, flames have been kept alive for days. These fires are maintained by residents to consume the garbage produced in the region. Trash collection around here was always irregular. It's a forgotten region. A stretch of land on a route only for the wretched. Dirt swept under the carpet. For it's under the carpet that these men live.

Residents don't feel the effect of the strike. They're used

to dispatching their own detritus; they live alongside black trenches, open pits, hidden quarries, automobile graves. They're used to remains.

And under new conditions, like these, some make themselves useful for some change. Jigs pass by, dragging garbage picked up from homes for fifty cents a wagonload. There are those who'll pay just for the convenience of not having to carry their garbage to the burn locations.

Edivardes pulls up next to a bus stop. This is where Alandelon gets off. From here, he'll travel for nearly two hours standing, holding onto a handrail, as he bumps along to his new workplace. And his body is prepped to bounce until it almost breaks.

Erasmo Wagner and his cousin continue. They see wagoners pulling small mountains of filth in continuous and silent streams along the shoulderless road, where dusty, treacherous tight curves, like conches, swallow men up whole every day. The stream of wagoners terminates in the flames of a burn. When they dump their trash, the fire is altered, intensifies in color, flickers rise and crackle in shorter intervals.

The farther they drive, the more intense, denser the black smoke becomes. The pavement is cleared, and the garbage collected, but the black smoke thickens above their heads. What is produced and then consumed spreads over the skies, but doesn't dissipate.

Erasmo Wagner ruminates calmly about how important his work really is. Important to the order, security, and health of society. Important to rats and vultures. Important to those who disparage it because of its acrid odor. More than a high-risk job, it's an indispensable profession. They fight for a fair wage, an adjustment that takes into account the insalubrious aspect of their work. Over the past months, accidents have driven workers out. Accidents never reported anywhere. Gunshots and criminal death are good to narrate. Great fatalities. Catastrophes. Scandals. But this work is perilous, and the frequency of accidents high. The man who touches something polluted becomes polluted, becomes as insignificant as trash. His accidents don't matter.

"So, I said to the woman," Edivardes recounts while driving, "you can give . . ."

"I wasn't paying attention to the beginning," interrupts Erasmo Wagner.

Edivardes drinks a little water from a blue bottle. Dries the sweat from his brow. Dry coughs. Hacks up phlegm, spits out the van window.

"I was saying when I opened the drain at home, I saw a handful of hair. I grabbed a stick and poked at it. It was a cat. It was still alive, bloody bastard. Its mouth was torn, its tail burned, and there was blood and pus mixed up with that stinking sink grease."

"But how'd the cat get there?" asks Erasmo Wagner.

"I also had no idea. That's when I called the woman and told her to take a look in the drain. She vomited right there," says Edivardes. "So I stuck my hand in the drain and plucked the cat out, sort of in pieces, and meowing softly."

"Someone put the cat there," reflected Erasmo Wagner.

"Exactly. The woman's husband. The guy didn't like her cat, and after mistreating it, stuck it in the drain. He was there too and ended up confessing."

"What did you do?" asks Erasmo Wagner.

"I got fucking mad. But it wasn't my problem. I cleaned the drain. It wasn't even that dirty, and told him to pay me. They were arguing, but I didn't care. I butted right in, got my cash, and left the cat dying on the living room rug."

They sit, taciturn. A dry and heavy silence. Erasmo Wagner spies Tonhão. The goat's peacefully chewing pages from the newspaper. He still doesn't understand how it got into the van, and he feels a strange burden. Erasmo Wagner knows this goat belongs to him, and carries him within, too. The way the goat confronts Erasmo Wagner makes him want to confess his sins. To redeem himself. A man like him feels redeemed by the suffering he's been through, the time he's done. But there are deeper layers of the soul, unreachable by human punishment or terrestrial disgrace. There's something in Erasmo Wagner that impels him to collect trash without questioning. It makes him want to disappear without a trace. He's never confessed, though he's devoted to some Catholic saints. At times, he feels the body is the soul's prison, even when he's out walking alone on the street. Ever since he saw Old Mendes's eyes in the goat's eyes, he's needed to confess. Tonhão is there to expiate Erasmo Wagner's sins, but he doesn't know it yet.

***

They leave Rosa Flor with the new goat owner. As for the buck, still no news from Mr. Aparício. For now, Tonhão will stay with Erasmo Wagner, but deep within, he knows he doesn't ever want to return the animal.

They stop at an old house situated beside a wooden pen containing a sounder of swine, chickens run loose about the yard, and there's a water cistern out back.

"We're here to wash out the cistern," says Edivardes.

"I've seen tanks blacker than a cesspool," says Erasmo Wagner.

A woman greets them and leads them out back. They pass a man who's checking out the pigs in the pigsty. They eye each other. The man has a calm, distant look.

"Make yourselves at home. I've left a bottle of water on the veranda if you get thirsty."

"Yes, ma'am," responds Edivardes.

"I'm seeing to some of the pigs I breed. If you need anything just holler."

The woman walks away to have a word with the man who's examining her pigs. Edgar Wilson has chosen three. He wants to take them immediately, but they need to negotiate a price, and for this, the pig butcher has all the time in the world.

Erasmo Wagner lifts the heavy asbestos cover from the tank. A bad smell reaches him from the silt and black waters in the cistern. It's lined with mud and the moss climbs up to and over the cover. The cistern hasn't been completely emptied for cleaning. Edivardes removes the plug from the bottom of the tank and lets the rest of the water and silt drain out.

Erasmo Wagner waits for the cistern to drain while he smokes a cigarette. He goes through the gate, and observes Tonhão, loose, on the other side of the street, grazing in an empty lot with some chickens. The pig dealer comes toward him and asks for a smoke. He gives him one. Edgar Wilson reaches for a box of matches in his pants pocket. The two stand quietly for two minutes, surrounded by light smoke.

"Do you like working with pigs?" Erasmo Wagner asks.

"They're good animals. They get used to us," responds Edgar Wilson.

The woman reappears and signals for Edgar Wilson to come speak with her. He says thanks for the cigarette, pays the woman, takes his three pigs, and goes away.

Erasmo Wagner puts the butt of his cigarette out on a stepping-stone and checks the cistern, now emptied of water. He climbs inside the tank and removes three dead pigeons, a faded blue sock, a yellow hair ribbon, a small spoon, and a AAA battery. He looks at the water bottle on the veranda and decides it's better to drench his thirst later with water from the street rather than from the spigot in the yard.

***

The stench of the city has become unbearable. Heat intensifies the acrid odor. People and rats share common space in broad daylight. They, the rats, walk free, and don't mind the sunlight. They scavenge trash, procreate on street corners, and amplify the horror of the scene with sharp, unclipped nails, which resound everywhere. The city has begun to rot. Once upon a time, it was thought violence would yield chaos, but now, in a matter of days, society's trash has produced putridness and calamity. Everyone's affected; everyone feels they're dragged through the muck. It only takes moments for a sardine tin, a disposable diaper, a Tetra Pak package, and a razorblade to spawn a mountain of filth in an active urban center.

Erasmo Wagner knows that whenever the sanitation strike ends, he'll have tons of work cut out for him. He'll have to collect in a single shift what's been accumulating for days. Seeing the garbage piled high all over the city, he's cognizant of how everything can go back to just being as it was. He was accustomed to collecting tons daily. He's used to lifting heavy bins, and the light spinal back pain that gradually increases, along with the obstacles, and the fatigue. But the tons that await are unknown tons. After a week, everything will be cleared, and the tonnage will again go unnoticed. So Erasmo Wagner still prefers rats and vultures; better the devil you know.

CHAPTER 6

Edivardes is paid for cleaning the cistern. Erasmo Wagner waits for his cousin in the van. Tonhão's in the back again, ruminating on grass from the pasture and chewing newspaper off the floor. Erasmo Wagner feels suddenly like a ruminant. He chews and rechews semi-digested recollections. Ruminatia are doomed to chew and rechew what they regurgitate into their mouths, and they're unaware; they ruminate without questioning.

Most of the men he knows are ruminants. And they do it in silence.

Edivardes gets behind the wheel and starts up the vehicle. Erasmo Wagner decides it's prudent to change the dressing on his hand. He's healing and the wound is drying out. The tooth he pulled is safely stored in a soap dish, and he can handle the other rotten tooth in his mouth. With the money he'll earn today for helping his cousin out, he'll treat his dental problems. He'll try to fix his smile, even though he smiles little.

It's a very hot day. They drink some warm water. Dry wind wafts in the windows and cracks their skin. But the heat makes them feel more alive; the excess makes them brutish. They'll continue along this road for six kilometers to *Dona Elza's Mandioca Frita*. They'll clean her grease trap. At least they'll be served a good lunch. Dona Elza likes to treat well those who do jobs for her. In her establishment, everyone eats, and around it, even the dogs are rewarded.

"It was on the radio. Seems the strike's almost settled," comments Edivardes.

Erasmo Wagner sighs. It takes him a minute to speak.

"We'll have double the work," says Erasmo Wagner. "It's all I think about."

"Do you suppose they'll reach a good agreement?"

"Good for whom?"

Erasmo Wagner feels the burden of an extended strike. He feels the weight of those extra tons accumulating as something they'll have to bear. He hears there've been fights, people got sick, rats proliferated, and the president of the republic made an appeal on TV. For Erasmo Wagner none of it matters. What does matter is seeing the city pure again, having his routine back, and following a trodden path.

The trip to the restaurant is rife with potholes; the shoulder is undefined because of high grass along the side of the road. There are no lights to navigate securely at night. There's no signage, but a lot of roadkill and tight curves. They pass a pickup stopped on the shoulder with hogs in the bed. A man waits to cross. They think they see a car wrapped around a tree. Erasmo Wagner lights another cigarette. He inhales smoke along with vapor from the heat of the day and Edivardes comments on a boxing match he watched on TV.

"I also saw it. The kid's angry. A fighter. But a cock without spurs," responds Erasmo Wagner.

He takes another sip of the warm water they carry in the van. Decides not to swallow, but rinses his mouth, and spits out the window. He recalls the pigs in the bed of the pickup. Life's full of ironies.

"Once I had a boss who wouldn't eat pork."

"Jewish?" asks Edivardes.

"He was black. Are there black Jews?"

"I've never met one."

"Me neither."

Erasmo Wagner attempts to open his window all the way, and has to bang on it to roll it down completely.

"It was a spiritual thing. He was religious," says Erasmo

Wagner. "And pork's impure in some religions."

"Yeah. I know."

"He'd always say: I wouldn't eat pork if you paid me. The animal's dirty. The meat's dirty. I don't like pigs."

Erasmo Wagner, with a faraway look, draws on a good memory.

"He'd repeat this portion from The Bible: "You must not eat their meat or touch their carcasses; they are unclean for you. Do not eat any detestable thing. God will destroy that person; for God's temple is sacred."

"So he was God's temple, huh?"

"He thought so. But the guy had a heart condition. One day he didn't show up for work, and he never missed a day. And then we learned he was in the hospital. Something wrong with his heart and he had an emergency operation."

Edivardes hits the brakes suddenly on a pothole. His head hits the roof of the van. The buck loses his balance and falls to one side. Erasmo Wagner reaches back and strokes Tonhão's head.

"He was in the operating room for hours. Woke up okay, recovered quickly, and later found out they'd replaced a valve in his heart."

Erasmo Wagner drags on the cigarette to the very last flare, then throws it out the window.

"So what?" says Edivardes.

"Doctors had put a pig valve in his heart."

Edivardes bursts out laughing. Erasmo Wagner, who laughs little, can't resist laughing along.

"Sonofabitch! Pig? A pig valve?"

Edivardes chokes he's laughing so hard.

"And so now he's better because of a pig. He has a piece of pig inside his chest making his heart beat."

Edivardes controls his laughter. Dries his mouth with his shirtsleeve. And after a few seconds of silence and relief, becomes serious again.

"What did he do, Erasmo?"

"He became depressed. Wanted to remove the valve from his heart. Wanted to die. And he did. From such distaste."

"God preaches the damnedest things," said Edivardes.

"God likes pigs. That's all. The man got a lesson."

"Yup . . . never underestimate a pig. Who knew . . . a pig valve in the heart?"

"He must have felt too impure to live."

In saying this, Erasmo Wagner thinks of his job. Edivardes maneuvers the van and parks in front of the restaurant.

***

Fossa, groove, trench; ground zero, pit; drainage ditch; cesspool; root, fossae. Faucet. Edivardes stares at the drain in the kitchen sink. He knows what's coming. Drain stench is old business. He sees a bubble form and, pop, it breaks. Sewage comes up the sinkhole. The stench is unbearable. Erasmo Wagner spies the drain. The scene repeats. He thinks of the ruminant and what comes up from the stomach into the mouth. The process is the same. The drain is the mouth and the sewer is the stomach. He's contemplative. Edivardes, standing next to him, is also. Before the next sewer bubble even bursts in the sink, they inhale the excrement.

The two walk in silence to the back of the restaurant, where they find the overflowing grease trap, and a sizeable concentration of filth. Edivardes holds the lid. He makes a face. He adjusts his cap and spits on the ground. It's a tenebrous thing to treat putrid excrement: Kala Azar, Cutaneous leishmaniasis, worms, Scabies, Schistosomiasis, Giardia, Typhus, Cholera, Bubonic plague.

The buried grease trap is made of concrete, and it holds 150 liters. The contents that drain from the sink find their way to the grease trap. It's where water and grease separate. When it cools off, the grease solidifies and forms blocks. It's necessary to reach into the trap and pull these blocks out by hand, and put them in a bag and throw them in the trash. Trash is what Erasmo Wagner should be collecting, if he weren't on strike; so, the hard-as-rock grease will have to keep, wrapped in plastic, until a collector comes by. This isn't on his route.

Erasmo Wagner takes off his shirt before helping his cousin remove the heavy lid. Addled cockroaches emerge from inside the trap. Cockroach eggs float on sheets of grease. Fat roaches drag their heavy selves along the floor. The buck bleats and rings his prized charm. Tonhão rubs its horns on Erasmo Wagner's legs. He yells an obscenity, and the goat runs to pasture on bushes at the back of the restaurant.

Edivardes grabs a black plastic bag from inside his knapsack. The two of them begin to remove solid floating fat.

"Do you know what today's plate of the day is?" asks Edivardes.

"No." Responds Erasmo Wagner.

"Fried pork crackling, collard greens, and polenta."

Erasmo Wagner doesn't feel like talking. He's focused on his work. He removes the plaques of fat and puts them in the large trash bag. He's thirsty, but he can't drink water now. He crouches lower and reaches as far as he can to grab the rest of the fat. But what looks like a floating piece of fat, broken off the larger block, catches his eye. Fuck, it's a piece of finger. A brown pinky with a massive fingernail.

Edivardes holds the finger up to the sun. Inspects it with care.

"But if it isn't a fucking finger!"

With a stick, Erasmo Wagner splashes the silt in the tank. Other fingers. All brown.

"I think we need to talk to Dona Elza," says Edivardes.

"If we tell her, it'll only be a headache," says Erasmo Wagner. "We've got a cesspit to clean two kilometers from here."

"Do I put it all in the bag?"

"Yes. It's not our problem, Edivardes."

"Do you think he lost his fingers in a bet?"

"I'd rather not know."

Erasmo Wagner sticks his hand into the tank and removes as many fingers as he can find. Ten in all. Despite being delicate members, he knows they dignify us. Without fingers, hands are just stubs. With no fingers, he couldn't collect trash. With no fingers he'd be the same as bucks, goats, and pigs. He'd be an ungulate mammal, with thick horny toes, an arthropod that can't pick up anything, only capable of sustaining its own weight. For some moments, the bagged fingers affect him. He hopes the person they belonged to is dead; otherwise he'll never again hold anything in his hands.

They finish the job. Clean up with a dribble of running water from a hose at the back of the yard. Water's scarce in these parts; that's why, when it's potable, it's worth gold. They check that sewage is no longer bubbling up through the sink, and are assured the stench will soon dissipate. They continue into the restaurant and order the plate of the day. Lunch is on the house. They don't see any fingerless black man. The men eating here all have fingers. They're missing teeth. As he thinks about this, his decayed molar wakes up, sharpened to a point, digging into the bone. Teeth can go missing, but for a man who depends on his arms to live, fingers are more essential. And they should be measured in muscular robustness and rapacity.

***

The days are on fire, peppered with a desperate stench. Erasmo Wagner receives the news of the end of the sanitations workers' strike with sadness. But, once they've worked like beasts of burden, the city will return to normal. The daily tons of filth, remains, and excrement will be familiar to his arms and loins. This comforts him.

They return home late at night, after cleaning out a septic tank. They stink; they're tired and contaminated. There's a breeze, which softens the rigidness of their moods after a sunny day. Edivardes stops the van at the side of the road to pee. This same dark road, full of potholes and lacking signage, but a full moon guides them. Erasmo Wagner decides to get out too. They relieve themselves on separate bushes. When they return to the van, the buck is no longer inside.

"Leave the goat," says Edivardes.

"I can't."

"What are you saying, Erasmo?"

"I'm going to look for it. The goat was in the car before we got out. It got out too, right here."

Edivardes is too tired to argue. He climbs into the van, grabs a flashlight from beneath the driver's seat and hands it to Erasmo Wagner. Without saying a thing, he pulls away in the van. When the red rear lights of the orange van disappear, Erasmo Wagner begins his search for the buck, hiding in brush along the side of the road.

He walks the length of the stretch of highway before heading into the woods. He lights a cigarette. He calls to the buck. He feels its hircus odor. He imagines it's not far off. Erasmo Wagner looks up at the sky. He passes his tongue over the roof of his mouth. He can't remember ever seeing so many stars. From the middle of that road, but few vestiges and traces are visible. Men and animals are quietly buried along the margins.

He hears Tonhão's distant bleating and chiming charm. He walks forward, but his only sound is the dry impact of his footsteps. He's worn out. It's been a hard day. He feels his back burn and his senses flicker. The flashlight's beam licks the scrub. The hircus odor increases. He wouldn't know how to explain what he's doing here, but certain things elude words. And for men like him, words make up a scarce vocabulary. He doesn't have the words to say much; in contrast, wordlessly, he's got sufficient soul and heart to express what he feels.

When he killed old Mendes, Erasmo Wagner was mute. But gazing into his eyes, he could tell the old man understood why he was dying. When he was released from jail, Erasmo Wagner found out that old Mendes was his dad. His aunt, who'd raised him, told him so. The man who'd raised him also knew the truth, but remained silent while Erasmo Wagner grew up.

He doesn't like to admit that the old goat was his father. Maybe that's why he needs to break the silence now. Ever since he saw old Mendes's eyes in the buck, he's felt the need to confess.

Tonhão's standing by a tree. Erasmo Wagner pulls the cord around his neck. The goat butts his horns against his legs, and he falls to his knees.

"What kind of devil are you, goat?"

Erasmo Wagner, kneeling, lowers his head. He turns off the flashlight and begins to whisper in the goat's ear. For Jews of the Old Testament there was an emissary goat, whose objective was to take on the burden of their confessed sins and transgressions and be cast out in the desert to disappear. Having read the Old Testament to his moribund aunt, he knew this story. And silently, in his own way, he yearned for a scapegoat to bring him to his knees somehow and, for once, relieve him of some of his burden.

The man speaks for a long time and when dawn brightens the night sky, he falls mute again. The buck walks off in the direction of the stream, carrying Erasmo Wagner's iniquities out of sight for absolute removal.

CHAPTER 7

Erasmo Wagner glues adhesive tape to the hood of his black raincoat before the rainfall increases. It's been a difficult afternoon. He's at the end of his shift. The garbage that's been accumulating for days requires extra work and this has meant overtime, a doubled workforce, and readjusted wages. Even after three days, when urban sanitation services have returned to normal, garbage is still piled high in out-of-the-way places. It'll take time to clean it all up. Dead rats grouped on top of garbage bags are thrown into the crusher. They wear facemasks to bear the stench as they dispose of the waste on their incessant route.

Valtair, the novice garbage collector, rolls a can in the direction of the truck, and Erasmo Wagner helps to turn its contents into the trash compactor. The strike led to modest wage adjustments, directed toward the insalubrious quality of their work. But the raise was minimal, and the risks are many. Most of the collectors are unsatisfied, but everyone else—who doesn't collect trash around the city—is very satisfied.

"Hadn't they banned these large bins?" asks Valtair.

"They had," responds Erasmo Wagner.

"Big cans destroy the spine. I feel a lot of pain when I lift one of these," explains Valtair.

The truck keeps traffic from flowing, and with the rain, everything becomes morose. A car stopped behind the truck honks its horn. Erasmo Wagner can't stand the sound of a car horn. The sound of the trash compactor, when turned on, grinds his nerves, but the car horns make him despair. The more they honk, the more they run, the quicker they hurl bags into the truck, but no one notices. Whoever is stopped behind the truck, immersed in the sour and rotten smell, can't stand the sound, and wants to move along. No doubt: the work they do is not for everyone. The woman in her car persists with her horn. After picking up a plastic container on wheels and throwing its contents into the mouth of the crusher, Erasmo Wagner turns on the compactor and walks toward the automobile. He knocks on the window. The woman is surprised. He knocks harder. She opens it.

He asks, "Do you know what we're doing here, ma'am?"

His face is soaked with rain. His smell is off. His eyes are gray. The woman hesitates, but speaks.

"You're collecting trash."

"Yes. This is our work: we collect your shit, because you, ma'am, can't do it yourself. That's what we're doing here."

The woman bites the corners of her lips.

"It's that I . . . it's that . . ."

"I'm sure you don't like anyone on your tail, ma'am, honking their horn, right?"

Erasmo Wagner fixes his gaze on the woman. She's pale and perfumed. A beautiful woman, incapable of collecting her own excrement, who just doesn't get the value of this work. A woman like most men. Erasmo Wagner turns his attention back to the job and runs behind the truck that's moved a few meters ahead.

Valtair's fighting with a dog over a bag of trash. Erasmo Wagner kicks the animal.

"You haven't learned, Valtair. You need to be alpha with the dogs. You need to make them understand you're boss. The dog sticks to the trash remnants, and not the trash, understood?"

Valtair understands; he's felt like a dog his whole life.

Erasmo Wagner climbs onto the tailgate of the accelerating truck, which will soon take a corner. Valtair appears a few meters back running with a trash bag in his hands. Erasmo yells for the truck to wait, but the driver doesn't wait for collectors. The collectors need to collect the trash, dump it in the crusher, and jump onto the tailgate of the truck in motion.

Valtair trips but doesn't fall. The truck doesn't reduce speed, but the kid manages to catch the tailgate anyway and grab ahold before turning onto the next street. And on this street there's more piled trash and traffic. The clap of thunder startles passersby; the clarity of a lightning bolt provokes a similar response. Erasmo Wagner would like to smoke a cigarette, but he'll have to wait two hours to do it. He looks at Valtair, who seems disoriented. A whiff of alcohol on his breath confirms his suspicions, but he doesn't say anything. Most collectors drink, maybe to put up with such waste, imperfection, disorder, and ruin. Erasmo Wagner doesn't drink. He faces everything with full consciousness; sobriety at all times, he prefers it that way.

The traffic begins to slowly move. The driver goes on to the yard. Erasmo Wagner looks back from the tailgate. His eyes are gray as the day, and his heart beats steadily, strong. He's still a silent man and feels capable of digesting the impurities, still marvels at everything around him. He's a man expunged, and yet he'll continue collecting the garbage of others, like a beast of burden, sterile, hybrid, unquestioning.

BOOK 3. *carbo animalis*

for dust you are / and to dust you will return.

—Genesis 3:19 (NIV)

CHAPTER 1

In the final accounting, what matters are teeth. They make identification possible. It's highly advisable for every individual to preserve their teeth above all else, even above dignity. Because dignity won't attribute what a person is, or rather, what they were. Vocation, finances, papers, memories, and love will have no bearing. When the body chars, only dentures will preserve the person's own, rightful story. A toothless sod has it worse than the most pitiful lout. For they'll become dust and charcoal. Nothing more.

Ernesto Wesley risks life and limb at all times. He throws himself into fire, crosses dense, black smoke, swallows sooty saliva, and can guess what material was used to make each item of furniture in every room based on how the flames crackle.

He can distinguish between cries of despair, blood, and death. At the beginning of his career, he learned that the business of saving another's life is made up of equal parts madness and determination. He wouldn't call himself a hero for his acts of bravery. At the end of the day, he feels the impact. He's determined to safeguard some faith in life, to make sure he gets up every morning and goes to work.

His failures are greater than his successes. He understands that fire is treasonous. It rises in silence, drags itself across surfaces, erases all vestiges, and leaves only ash. Anything a person builds or attains can be devoured in a single licking. Everyone is within reach of the flame.

Ernesto Wesley doesn't like to respond to the call of

automobile or airborne accidents. He doesn't like torqued iron, and having to saw through it even less. The emergency rescue saw makes him uncomfortable. Plunge cutting through metal can give him the rushing quivers, and he might lose control. It makes his body rigid and robotic. The slightest error could be fatal. Make a mistake in a profession like his, and become a condemned villain. Putting himself at risk is par for the course. It's what this is about. He's trained to save lives; but if he fails, a disapproving glance can turn his honor to ash.

The only good fight there is—fire. He likes to dodge blazes and outrun violent flames that rise on an abundance of oxygen. He'll rake his stomach along a floor to feel the heat come through his uniform: wallboard caving around him, one floor crashing onto another, wires dangling, walls breaking. The sputtering of flames measures his resistance over time, and reminds him of the imminence of death. But there's nothing that compares to that feeling of carrying someone on his back, a weight greater than his own, a rescued person who'll never again forget his darkened, soot-covered face.

Ernesto Wesley is the best at what he does, but few know it.

He smiles at the bathroom mirror and pulls floss through his teeth. He carefully cleans the deep crevices and finishes his ablutions with a mint-flavored mouthwash. His teeth are clean. Few cavities. One molar has a gold cap. He melted down his deceased mother's wedding ring to make a crown for his tooth. This is for identification, in case he dies at work, or in any other circumstance. It's uncommon to have a gold tooth, and it will make it easier for them to identify him.

"How's Oliveira?" asks a man at the urinal.

"They say he's well," responds Ernesto Wesley, "but they had to amputate his hand."

"Hell!"

The man finishes at the urinal and moves to the sink. He glances at his hands and sighs. The running water comes in a thin beige stream.

"This faucet's still broken," says the man.

"It's not the faucet. There's little water here."

"The water's filthy."

"It's the old pipes. Everything's old."

"It makes me feel older. Did they find Guimarães's dentures?"

"I looked through the rubble, but didn't find them."

"How'd they identify the body?"

"A birthmark on his foot. That foot remained practically intact for identification."

"Without teeth, it takes a stroke of luck like that."

"Guimarães was blessed. Six bodies destroyed and still unidentified. And another coworker missing."

"I know . . . Pereira."

"Now, only when the forensic team liberates him."

"Pereira had small pointed teeth."

"They were awful, a mess of cavities."

The two men look at each other through the bathroom mirror; they silently take in the unsettling hum of the fluorescent light that crackles every now and again, as if to say it might burn out any second.

"It'll be those ugly little teeth that save him now," says Ernesto Wesley.

"Right. I could identify Pereira from those teeth myself."

"Shark teeth."

The bathroom door opens. A short man with a penetrating stare enters holding a clipboard.

"You'll both need to attend to this horror."

Ernesto Wesley finishes up at the urinal and zips his fly.

"Collision. Two cars and a truck. People pinned in the metal."

"Fredrick's good on the power saw."

"He's off today. You two are all we've got."

"How many victims?"

"Six."

"Drunks?"

"Two."

"Makes me feel like a fucking trash collector," mutters Ernesto Wesley, who's been mum so far.

"That's all it is," says the man.

The two men follow him out to the pickup truck. The incident is five kilometers away on the highway.

"I want a smoke," says Ernesto Wesley.

"Me too. I don't know how you manage white teeth."

"I bleach them with baking soda."

"You have the best teeth in the group, Ernesto. And you have the best incisors I've seen on anyone. A perfect rectangle that leaves a distinct bite on a sandwich."

"You've noticed."

"I and the whole gang. I can tell when a leftover sandwich is yours by the bite."

The man, impressed, adjusts his seatbelt until he hears the *click*.

"I don't like sawing. It makes me hyperconscious," murmurs Ernesto.

"Maybe we won't need to."

Ernesto Wesley looks up at the sky. It's full of stars and the moon hasn't appeared yet. He extends his gaze and cranes his head, but doesn't find it.

"Unlikely. Something tells me I'll use a rescue saw today," Ernesto Wesley comments.

"I hate drunks," says the man.

"Me too," Ernesto Wesley agrees.

"My sister was killed on the road heading up to Colinas, seems like yesterday."

"I remember that. Had to pull a guy out of the metal. Bald bastard."

"He cut her in half."

"I remember that too."

"At the time, I wanted to kill the bastard. I was this close to killing the guy."

"We're paid to save even the most bastardly, bald, and drunken sons of bitches."

"I'm tired of irresponsible shit."

"We've got to learn to live with the stench of irresponsible shit. That's what we're paid to do," concludes Ernesto.

Ernesto Wesley lowers his head, resigned. His eyes burn, tear up, but he hasn't cried in three years. Hasn't been able to. Ever since, his tears evaporated.

Silence rises over the men. They're tired, but they've learned to act on impulse. They know their limits, their extensive limits. The highway follows a river, and Ernesto Wesley squints to see the horizon beyond the filthy, turgid freshwater, his eyes narrow in vain searching for some direction or destination; but it's not always possible to reach for what the eye can't see. Ernesto Wesley is a bruiser with wide shoulders, a deep voice, and a square chin, however, this becomes minor once you notice his eyes. They're deep-set, black, and they shine intensely. But not with a glimmer of joy, rather the glint is of fires fought, and often admired. When he crosses a fire barrier that shines in his eyes, everything's scorched. His soul's set afire and his breath reeks of coal dust.

By the time he turned sixteen, Ernesto Wesley had witnessed fires in four homes where he lived. His laid-back family was powerless against flames slyly sparked in some odd room of the house. They were never gravely injured. The last time, he saved his older brother, Vladimilson, who got trapped inside when a door jammed. Ernesto Wesley was then horrified by fire, and spooked easily when confronted by the mildest source of heat or blast of hot air. But, when he ran back into that house to rescue his brother, he got burned for the first time. Oddly that day he learned flames don't hurt. There's no pain or ardor. He carried the unconscious Vladimilson on his shoulders, and never again missed a chance to be on the fire-frontline.

Ernesto Wesley doesn't feel flames burning his skin. He has congenital analgesia, a rare condition that affects his central peripheral nervous system. It makes him impervious to burn, stab, and puncture wounds. Ever since that first time, he's come to have an insatiable taste for fire.

He hid his condition from the Fire Corps; maybe if they knew the risks he ran they'd never have let him in. He walks on fire, under burning columns, and is lapped at by flames. He burns, but doesn't feel it.

Few people with this condition reach adulthood. He's covered in purple bruises.

He learned to pat his body down to see if any bone is out of place. He's broken his legs, ribs, and fingers. Ernesto Wesley is attentive to his own body and considers the condition something more than a clinical pathology: he sees it as a gift.

Lacking the pain sensation, his courage has grown thick and it takes him where no man will go, or maybe just a few others.

He makes regular medical appointments to examine his body and keep his health in check. He's convinced he can withstand greater trials than others. However, there's one kind of pain to which he's not impervious: heartache. In stark contrast to his condition, he suffers repeatedly. The pain of loss profoundly mortifies him. Red and yellow lights reflect in the middle of the highway. Two policemen signal for cars to continue in a single file. They stop and get out.

At a distance, Ernesto Wesley sees a knot of metal where two cars and a truck collided. Merged. They'll have to work harder than he'd imagined. He puts on special overalls, extrication gloves, a welding helmet, and he picks up a chainsaw to extract victims from the wreckage. He waits to be signaled. Other first responders arrived earlier at the site. Ernesto Wesley will need to "peel and peek." It's what they say when pulling the steel apart.

"Five victims, or rather six. Three trapped in the wreckage, including a dog. Two more have been taken to the hospital," says a rescue worker from the first team.

Ernesto Wesley checks the status of cars and truck. The truck driver's the only one not to suffer injury. He's standing, close to the firemen, trying to help. This is his fifth accident and he's escaped unscathed from all of them. A square sign tacked to the truck worries firefighters. It says Flammable Liquid. Chemical explosion followed by fire is one of the most hellacious evils to survive. A firefighter performed a check and found no risk of leakage. Ernesto Wesley pulls on the starter cord to start the rotary saw and hears no more moans, sirens, or anything else of the sort. He's immersed in the anesthetic impact of the rescue saw and the shrill friction of the blade against steel knots.

The only thing that pleases Ernesto Wesley about the hard work of cutting and separating are the random sparks released in the air, dancing nervously. Some do not fly up, but instead fall and touch the ground.

A five-year-old girl is trapped and awake. Her Labrador is crushed on her lap. The animal's blood on the girl's face, and all the while she calls to the dog. It'll be necessary to engage it with the car parts; the problem is the trauma this will cause the girl. He'll first have to cut off the dog's head and then its limbs. If it weren't for the dog, the girl would be dead. Ernesto Wesley can't be affected by this. He needs to cut down the trees. He feels heartache whenever he has to rescue a child, but his personal pain doesn't matter to anyone. This profession won't allow for dwelling on individual tragedy. It's above all an activity that greatly strengthens character by putting a person in the worst situations. The weight of things becomes relative when facing death. Not a peaceful, sleepy death, but a death that shatters, disfigures, and tears human beings apart piece by piece. Crumbling skulls, crushed and severed limbs. When a shock victim realizes his foot is two meters away, or his leg has fallen into the gap separating highway lanes, he'll never forget it. It's okay to lose: love, money, respect, dignity, family, title, or status; all can be regained. But nothing will replace a severed limb.

He engages the blade with the dog's head and car panel. Blood and steel splatter. The girl's in shock. It takes two hours but she survives and crawls out of the rubbish holding a paw. The girl's rescue has been emotionally wrenching, but her parents' rescue will be worse.

Her father will lose body parts if Ernesto doesn't concentrate. The heavy rain that's been coming down for some forty minutes and soaked through his overalls makes it more difficult. The men are weary. Few onlookers remain at the scene.

Most fatigued of all is Ernesto Wesley. And this becomes evident when the power saw trembles in his hand, wobbles between the vehicle's wheels, and touches the man's calf. He stops. Takes a deep breath. Looks around. He's been sawing for five hours.

"This man should be replaced," orders the officer in charge of the operation.

Another safety firefighter, who was assigned with Ernesto Wesley to the car, is told to take over on the power saw. After donning his protective uniform, he taps Ernesto Wesley on the shoulder.

"Now it's me. Go get some rest. You look terrible, man."

"I told you I hate sawing. I've got such a headache."

When the fireman tries to remove the girl's mother, she's already dead. Her pulse is easy to check, her head is reclined on the back seat, next to an open window. He cuts for an additional hour. Sparks fly every now and then. And when there's flammable liquid leaking nearby and no one notices, it's generally fatal. The worst thing in this profession is how one man's mistake affects all others. The firefighter on the rotary saw is thrown across the highway divide while Ernesto Wesley swallows a painkiller near the ambulance. The man on fire zigzags the high sky in the early morning. He feels his skin shrivel, his hair scrunch up, and as he hits the pavement still alert, he hears his bones crack on impact with the flames, rapidly inflaming his bowels. As he becomes char, he senses the mighty burning rankness of his own skin, muscle, nerve, and bone.

His teeth were intact and even the examiners agreed: they were the best incisors they'd ever seen on a dead man.

CHAPTER 2

Fat acts as a combustive and increases the intensity of fire. As such, a thin person takes longer to be reduced to ash than a fat one. The crematorium fire reaches 1000 degrees. Even teeth have difficulty resisting the unendurable white heat. The line of bodies to be cremated is eternal. They remain frozen until they bake in the ovens, and their stony remains are ground down into uniform, smooth, granular ashes.

While a body is being carbonized, its extremities contort and scrunch up. Anything that was once human seems to retreat to the insides. The mouth gapes and contracts. The teeth spring out. The face wilts into a pendulous yowl of horror.

Ronivon passes a mobile metal detector over the atrophied chest of an old man before closing his coffin. It's a necessary measure, in the case of a pacemaker, to prevent the high-heat furnace from exploding.

The machine beeps and a small signal blinks. It's been defective like this for weeks. He put in a request for a new one, but it hasn't been ordered yet. Ronivon shakes the machine and taps it a few times. The green light comes on, indicating it's working again.

The old man died of pulmonary complications. He'd been a smoker for forty-seven years. The old geezer has basically been slowly cremating over time. Of his lungs, only a piece of the left one remains. His jaundiced skin is wrinkled to the extreme, and looks like snake hide. His creases are deep. The tips of his fingers are stained by smoke to a caramel color. A body so thin and dry as his will take extra time to burn. The next coffin in line belongs to a forty-eight-year-old woman. Pretty face. Straight, black hair. Cause of death: heart attack—unusual for a woman. On the roster, there are still six more bodies to be cremated today.

The charnel furnace measures 3 meters wide, 2.6 meters long, and 2.4 meters tall. This retort model can hold two individual bodies at the same time. So, it renders greater service and, since they traded the old one out for this new model, Ronivon perceives it's given him the advantage at work. His lunch hour is twelve minutes longer due to the upgrade.

Open the little oven door and insert the coffins, each on its own shelf. Regulate the temperature to 1000 degrees and verify the time. Insert bodies in the oven while it's still cold. Sit on a plastic bench and leaf through a magazine borrowed from reception.

Not everyone knows that two bodies are cremated simultaneously. The "coal-maker," the workers' nickname for the retort, is in the basement. On the floor above, relatives wait patiently in ecumenical ceremony rooms where they watch over the deceased prior to cremation. A farewell lasts fifteen minutes. Ronivon believes men should return to dust; from dust they were made. He doesn't believe in final ashes. For him, it's necessary to return all the way to pulverized dust. Ashes are subversive. Remains are still recognizable, at least in the laboratory. Skeletal bits of bone, remnants of organic tissue, hair, and other things are long-lasting evidence. Better than leaving ash is to leave no trace at all. Leave no tomb, or posthumous memorial flowers, and no beloved person to visit. Ash might still be recognizable in a lab, but when pulverized to dust, those remains are no longer identifiable, whether human or animal.

Through the chamber viewport, he observes the body of the woman being thoroughly consumed, as he'd imagined it would be. The old man, parched like bark, doesn't seem to have suffered any alteration. It'll be a long cremation.

In the columbarium, the place urns are deposited, there are

always a few left behind. For lack of space, the crematorium must daily dispense of two or three urns held for relatives of the deceased that have passed the mandatory thirty-day window for recovery. Norms and regulations are clearly posted at the reception, nailed to a board where they should be read and executed:

—Written authorization must be completed before the crematory can accept remains for cremation

—Receipt of payment is necessary for the presentation of cremated remains to the family to be taken away

—Recovered ashes are made available 2 hours after cremation

—Rooms are available for 15-minute farewell ceremonies

—All bodies must be identified by a family member prior to cremation

—All ashes will held in the columbarium for a maximum period of 30 days

Beneath this, in tiny letters, it says: in the case of abandoned cremains, crematory staff will respectfully spread or inurn them for perpetual care at the base of rose bushes in the well-manicured scattering gardens. Manicured in the part meant for relatives to disperse the mortal remains of their beloved departed. Out back, in the high forest, wilted flowers and mounds of flies line stinking ditches where these cremains flow into a stream that leads to the sewers. It's precisely to these sewers that ashes from the charnel house go. What was once human is respectfully thrown in with the feces.

We die, we're burned until our bones are toast, ground into uniform grains, and thrown into the sewers by strangers. The ecumenical act is for others. The dead wait for their ashes to turn to dust. And, for the less fortunate, there's the filth of sewer-graves.

It's simple work. So long as you like fire and can deal with heat; it's non-stressful. The client never complains, and in the case of damaged merchandise, all that's needed is to fill a funereal urn with some ash surplus kept by the coal-maker maintenance crew. Grab a few fistfuls of prevenient ashes over the course of many cremations, and put them in a plastic gallon bucket. Later grind them down uniformly and use them in the case of others' lost grains.

The door opens and the supervising cremationist enters snacking on a biscuit. His name is Palmiro. He was blinded in one eye, when a spark neglectfully hit it. He doesn't use a patch. He prefers to expose the blind eye. White globe where there should be black. It tears a lot, and dilated veins give it a frightening aspect. Ronivon has learned to avoid looking at the blind eye.

"Ronivon, how are these doing?"

"More or less well. I've got a wispy bark-like old guy."

"Bad luck."

"Yeah. What's more, he was a smoker."

"I remember the type from when I was cremator. The body's used to fire and heat. It can resist a long time."

"Unfortunately I still have six more bodies, don't think I'll be able to go tonight."

"But playing cards is no fun if you're not there. Look, you've got six bodies but only three burns."

"I'm pretty sure this brittle old man's going to drag out my day."

"There were so few people at his funeral. No one was even upset."

"By the looks of it, someone's going to have to put the guy's ashes in the stream out back."

Palmiro sighs and lowers his head. This end is sad. He's usually the one responsible for throwing cremains in the stream. Ronivon rises, verifies the retort temperature, checks the gears; sees that the old man has begun to cede to the fire.

"The game's our religion."

"I know, Palmiro. It just depends on what time I can get out of here."

"Then I hope the coal-maker burns hotter than hell."

Palmiro slams the door as he leaves. He walks slowly through the long corridor in the direction of the stairs. He's a stocky man with few hairs on his head, and a tremulous quality. Having worked so many years in the coalpits and, years hence, cremating bodies, his lungs are broken down. His breathing is noisy and he's constantly coughing up phlegm into tissues he stuffs in his pants pockets. Before reaching the stairs he turns around and goes back to the retort room. He sticks his head in the door.

"Are you taking care of the pulverizing too, Ronivon?" he yells.

"Yes. I'll need to grind them all afterward. All alone today."

"Don't worry—I'm going to send J.G. to help you. He can grind."

Ronivon stretches. He's thirsty. He drinks four liters of water a day in this heat. His lungs are wearing out due to the shock of cold water in his hot body. He rises and grabs his blue jacket from behind the door. Embroidered above the left-side breast pocket are the words *Colina dos Anjos*.

He walks to the staffers' bathroom at the end of the hall. He splashes water on his face and checks his teeth. He's got excellent teeth.

Before working in the charnel house basement, Ronivon had worked below ground in an old building that was headquarters to an artisanal soap factory. There, he spent hours stirring a large pot of boiling fat. Unlike coal, it smelled of excrement, suet, and waste. His eyes would remain fixed on a swirl of glycerin, fatty acid, fat, lard, and bacon.

The factory was unfit for rats, and as he worked he wondered how he'd escape if the building collapsed. There were enormous cracks, gaps that stretched from ceiling to floor, hosting all sorts of insects. Those working in the basement wouldn't have a chance if everything came crashing down. There was the weight of six floors suspended overhead, and who knows what else they kept up there. After four years stirring that boiling pot of fat, he's now spent another five cremating corpses in this basement. One more year completes a decade that Ronivon has spent more of his time at the level of the inhumed than above. The sun is a stranger to him. He's pale. He's become accustomed to being beneath ground, and to fire.

He takes a sip from the water fountain next to the bathroom and returns to the furnace room. J.G. is standing there, looking sidewise at the retort.

"Mr. Palmiro sent me to grind the remains," says J.G.

"There are two behind this door."

J.G. eyes the door and gives the sacred charm around his neck a squeeze. Ronivon understands the lad's fear of grinding mortal remains. He'd like to help but someone needs to grind the coal-maker remains, as someone needs to grind toast for breadcrumbs.

J.G. is a large, black youth, and he weighs tons. Little is known about his life, but in fact J.G. has little life to remember. It was all repetition. Bodily scars are memories of his mother. As a child, he and his little sister were regularly abused. The most visible scar is the one on his lower lip, a gap that left his mouth deformed.

One day, his mother, coming in from work in a bad mood, takes it out on the kids. The youngest can't withstand the beating this time. She collapses on the floor next to the dog bowl. J.G. survives only because his mother notices the little girl isn't responsive to her blows any longer. That's when she stops hitting them and comes to the help of the children. When J.G. is released from the hospital, his mother is in jail. He never saw her again. In lieu of his mother, aunts and others raised him. But he rarely knew what degree of consanguinity he had with these relatives.

He learned to respond promptly to their orders and to say: yes sir, yes ma'am, and I'm sorry—even when it wasn't his fault. And his smile is brief due to his crippled lip.

The only thing J.G. accumulates in life is fat. His fat is the inverse of all his losses, sorrows, and suffering. He walks with difficulty. His body has folds. His arms don't reach his back.

His chest groans when he breathes. His voice is deep and slow. Across his skin there are dark stains and stretch marks.

After years of continuous beatings he's feebleminded. He never learned to read and write. His reasoning is as brief as his smile, and as deformed as his mouth.

"J.G. behind this door you'll find two dry branches."

"Mr. Ronivon, sir, aren't you afraid to burn these people?"

"They already died. It's just their remains. What do we make here, J.G.?"

J.G. looks upward and seems to find understanding in the peeling ceiling.

"Charcoal. We make charcoal."

Ronivon pats J.G.'s arm and smiles.

"Exactly. We make charcoal."

"I like barbecue, Mr. Ronivon. We use charcoal in our barbecue."

"Of course you do. But not this kind of charcoal."

"No. From this charcoal we make the ash that goes in the garden."

J.G.'s smile widens. Whenever he talks about the gardens that border the crematorium lot and the fruit-laden guava trees, fruit he loves to eat, his smile extends.

"Rose bushes like charcoal dust."

"Yes, J.G., they do."

"I care for the roses. I take good care of them. I like it here, Mr. Ronivon."

"I know."

"But I think I can't sleep in the little room anymore."

"Why, J.G.? Are they kicking you out?"

"A new janitor's coming to live in my little room. That's the condition, the crematory boss says so."

J.G. lowers his head and whimpers.

"We'll figure this out, okay?"

"My Auntie Madeleine hit me and called me demented. I don't want to go back to her house. She used a bedpan and I had to empty it every day. Here nobody hits me and there's no bedpan."

J.G. hiccups as he speaks.

"We'll find a place for you to stay," says Ronivon, stirred.

"Thanks. You're a good man."

"Enough. Go grind the charcoal. There'll be two more coming out of the retort."

"Yes sir, on my way."

He enters the grinding room and closes the door with the peace of mind to consider how he'll sprinkle the ashes resulting from his work at the foot of the rosebushes, and maybe he'll have a new place to sleep.

The employee that takes care of refrigerated bodies pushes a cart into the room with the next in line.

"Hey . . . you're lucky today."

Ronivon walks over to his coworker and checks the body on the gurney. He raises an inquisitive eyebrow. The coworker smiles.

"Check it out. Shortcut. This fireman was burnt in an explosion."

Ronivon just sighs, resigned.

CHAPTER 3

It seems like day hasn't dawned yet. It's very cold and the sky is covered in lumpy clouds. Steam from his warm breath suggests it's going to be a hard winter. This rarely occurs. Ernesto Wesley puts on all the jackets he can find in the closet, since he has no cold resistance. He drinks the hot coffee that his brother, Ronivon, made before leaving for work. Ernesto has the night shift, so he takes advantage of a free morning to care for his worm farm, at the back of the yard. It takes a great deal of his time.

Ernesto Wesley has an original 1974 red and white Lambretta scooter, which he's mechanically overhauled and updated with new tires. He bought it three years ago, at a nearby family estate sale. He sold a lawnmower and a water pump to buy it. He walks over to the garage, a simple, asbestos-cement tile lean-to at the side of the house, and finds the Lambretta, just as he left it, protected under a yellow tarp.

On the street, before starting the engine, he grabs a wool cap with ear protectors and a pair of gloves from his pocket. At sixty kilometers per hour, Ernesto Wesley heads to a farm eighty kilometers from his home. The bleak route is surrounded by hills. Some stretches are better conserved, and on his journey he passes cattle-drawn carts, people on foot, other scooters, and a few buses. Mostly it's solitary and partially quiet. This pleases Ernesto Wesley who moves rhythmically along with the Lambretta's motor. Its strident sound dulls the fire-engine sirens that periodically screech in his head and keep him alert. For Ernesto, there's never any real peace and quiet.

The region is cut through by contaminated rivers and small pastures. A human landscape mixes with the semi-rural. On average, there's a neighborhood every three kilometers. They're small urban areas with confused circulation, sprawling commerce, and minimal signage. People, cars, bicycles, drunks, children, pigs, and caged chickens crisscross on the same road, which at dangerous intervals displays a skull and crossbones to mark the high incidence of fatal accidents. For death is a constant on this road, like a long black vein. A clandestine outcropping at the foot of a mountain range.

He enters the farm through an iron gate and proceeds to the sugarcane mill. A short, fat man feeds cane, one stalk at a time, into the manual grinder. Another guy, tall and slim, turns the lever with enough strength to press the cane, leaving only the bagasse.

"Morning," says Ernesto, coming to a stop on his scooter.

"Morning," responds the fat man.

"I came to get cow manure."

"Mr. Gervásio is over there with the cows."

Ernesto nods in thanks and continues on the Lambretta to the next field. When he spies Gervásio, he turns off the motor, and walks up to him.

"Ernesto, son, how are you?"

"Well, Mr. Gervásio. And you, sir? And the family?"

The man ponders for seconds. He masticates, since it doesn't appear that he's eating anything. So much time spent with cows, Mr. Gervásio has picked up their habit of ruminating. He frequently looks consternated and wears a five o'clock shadow, exactly two centimeters of beard. It's as if the man groomed his beard to look that way. After ruminating for one or two more seconds, he decides to speak.

"My cows are well. The pasture's good too," he says formally, gazing out to infinite space. His eyes always stare beyond what others can see.

"My eldest daughter's getting married," he says solemnly, his eyes adjusting to the moo of a cow that grazes nearby.

"Congratulations," says Ernesto.

Gervásio shakes his head.

"Every time someone speaks about this wedding my cows moo. It's jinxed. I think Dolinha is making a bad choice. He's a doctor. I don't like doctors. But she won't listen. She won't listen to the cows. She only has ears for the doctor," finishing this speech, he ruminates again in silence.

"Mr. Gervásio, I've come for manure."

"And how are your worms, son?"

"They're well . . . they like the manure from your cows very much. They've become really glossy."

"My manure's the best in the region. People come from far away to buy it. When the cow's good, even its shit is valuable."

The man turns to one of his farmhands. He's slight and cross-eyed and has a speech impediment. When he says something, it comes out twangy and high-pitched.

"Zeca, bring Ernesto's manure over, and the bag I've put aside there too."

He turns toward Ernesto, his face softening as he finds silence again. They wait quietly for the manure to be brought over. The foggy morning seems colder in open pasture. There are signs of a light frost on the plants' leaves. Mr. Gervásio calmly takes out his pipe, and rests it in the corner of his mouth. He takes a pinch from a roll of tobacco he keeps in the pocket of his flannel shirt, and with a worn-out little knife, useless for cutting, shaves the pinch of tobacco, putting the shavings in his pipe. He returns the tobacco and knife to his pocket, and lights the pipe with the flick of a match.

"We're going to have one of those winters," comments Ernesto Wesley.

"It's true. I need to take care with the cows more than ever."

"They say it'll be the worst winter in thirty years."

"That's what it seems like. I don't remember this kind of cold."

The nasal-sounding boy brings the two bags on his shoulders, and lays them at Ernesto Wesley's feet.

"Ernesto, today I want to give you a sample of Marlene's shit. Marlene's the cow under that tree over there. This cow produces some of the best manure I've seen in my life."

Mr. Gervásio kneels down and opens the bag. He proudly reveals its contents.

"It's simultaneously dense and smooth. The smell is strong and sour. I want to give you a little bit of Marlene's manure for you to test with your worms. But use it in a separate part of the worm factory. Two weeks from now you'll begin to see a difference. Marlene's shit is so precious, I've not even put a price on it yet."

"Oh, Mr. Gervásio, thank you, sir. I'll use it today."

"You won't regret it. My son hasn't even seen this batch yet. He's out west in Rio das Moscas."

"Has he gone boar hunting?"

"Yes, I don't know when he'll be back. It's a plague of boars out there. The beasts are devastating everything."

"Maybe one day I'll drum up the courage to go after one myself."

"Courage? Courage's something you don't lack for, kid."

Ernesto picks up the bags and sets them on the Lambretta. He ties them tight so they won't fall off. The bigger bag he ties behind him, where he carries a spare, and the other up front, under his feet. He pays the man, and says goodbye. On the Lambretta, Ernesto makes two quick stops in specialty stores to buy tools, sunflower seeds, and other things he needs, and then he goes home.

***

When she was just a pup, a board fell on her, while she was eating, and crushed Jocasta's cranium. It was a small incident that would've passed by unnoticed, had it not been for some pained growls. Though normality has never been part of the bitch's life, her behavior changed dramatically. She became more agitated and neurologically perturbed. Opening and closing her mouth every five seconds was one of the first symptoms. Slobbering from the corner of her mouth and an eternal puppy look were others. On the other hand, this mental disturbance gave her more courage and boldness. Jocasta has no fear of fire or water. She's capable of chasing a lion and hunting down leopards. She's a nice looking dog with a stiff yellow coat, a wagging tail, ears lightly fallen at the points, svelte musculature, and an elegant gait. She likes to trot through the yard, imperiously.

During a storm, she'll run from one end of the yard to the other barking at the lightning. Lightning leaves her furious. When she barks at it, it's as if she were discussing abundantly with God. Her acts sometimes confer divinity. On sunny days, she chases her own shadow. Sometimes she spends interminable hours in pursuit of her shadow, which she's not been able to catch yet. Although she can't catch her own shadow, she catches all the insidious rats that walk almost unsuspectingly through the yard at night. Jocasta takes care of the worm farm like a dog that takes care of her own litter. She's sterile like a beast of burden, and will never have any pups of her own, but she's got lots of worms for which she cares. Every day she deposits the spoils of a night spent in alert—generally five or six dead rats, at Ernesto and Ronivon's back door. She insists on putting them there since it's the first door that opens in the morning, and it's important that her owners see the results of her work when they wake. Her disturbance gives her another skillset: a rare ability to find the early nuclei of anthills in formation. She'll stop next to one and spin around her tail various times. But of all activities she most likes to frighten the neighbor's chickens when they jump over the fence. They come to her side of the yard to attempt to rake up her portly worms in captivity.

Ernesto Wesley arrives home with bags of cow manure and throws a handful of sunflower seeds to Jocasta, for that shiny, glow-in-the-sun fur coat. Jocasta lies comfortably in her pile-of-rags bed in the improvised garage and quietly chews on the seeds before taking a nap.

Ernesto Wesley raises red Californian worms. These worms prefer animal manure and are excellent in the production of humus, which is nothing more than worm shit resulting in a substance that looks like coffee grounds. The humus he sells to some small farmers, gardeners, landscapers, and anyone who wants fertile soil in their home gardens. He sells some worms live as fishing bait and others dehydrated. On sunny days early in the morning he puts the worms in a plastic bag to expose them to the sun. Once exposed to heat they evaporate moisture and dehydrate; on days in which there's no sun, he puts them in the oven. It's not unusual for him to make pizza next to a pan full of worms.

Sitting at the table he takes a sip of coffee and eats two dry pieces of toast before going to work in the yard. Today he'll feed the worms, and prepare the vermicomposting. The coffee's hot and it helps him keep warm. His nose is cold. He rubs his hands on his pants for the warmth friction provides. He notices a white envelope on the dish cabinet. He reaches back and gently inclines his chair until he can reach it. Together with the sealed envelope is a note from his brother Ronivon.

Ernesto this arrived yesterday.

It's for you again.

Now it's one per week.

He looks at the letter and puts it on the table. He taps his fingers lightly on it. He feels his heart constrict. He thinks about opening it. He puts his fingers against his eyes, closes them, and remains like this for some time. When he needs to make mental effort, Ernesto Wesley closes his eyes and presses his thumb and indicator finger against his eyelids. He's irked. He drinks the rest of the coffee in his cup, leaves the sealed envelope on the table, and heads into the yard.

Ernesto removes layers of the shirts he's wearing, leaving the cap on his head, and he changes the wool gloves for a pair of leather gloves. He approaches the compost; a meter-high pile of decomposing organic matter that's been fermenting for a week, and he begins to turn it. It smells of rot. It contains leftover food, fruit, paper scraps, dried leaves, and grass cuttings. Ronivon prepared the pile and left this second stage for Ernesto. When the temperature of the mass nears ambient temperature, it's the ideal moment to add it to the worm farm. And this is that moment. He puts the manure and the compost in the worm bed. Apparently there are no signs of ants or other plagues.

The neighbor, Dona Zema, approaches the yard fence and yells his name. He stops his work to go to the woman.

"Morning, Dona Zema."

"Morning, Ernesto. It's that I really need to talk to you and I haven't found you or your brother."

"How can I help?"

"It's that your bitch has been playing havoc with my hens. Just last week, two of them were injured and one ended up dying. She'd just laid eggs in the nest and the eggs were abandoned so I had to finish the job myself."

"You sat on the eggs, Dona Zema?"

"With the help of God—right?—we do it all. You know the money from those hens and their eggs is what puts food on my table."

"Yes I know it, ma'am."

"My life is full of sacrifice. I'm alone in everything I do."

"Yes, ma'am."

"I want you to do something about that dog. She's costing me damages. She's soft in the head, everyone knows."

"Dona Zema, the thing is, your hens have been jumping the fence to dick around after my worms. Jocasta's only been doing her job—she's been taking care of the worm factory."

"I don't know, Ernesto. That bitch is spoiled. And some days she gets in my yard."

"In your yard? Are you sure it's my dog? Because Jocasta's

good at what she does over here. She catches rats, finds anthills, and chases your chickens away when they jump the fence."

"Look Ernesto, I'm asking nicely now. But if your bitch gets at my hens again, she'd better watch out. Cause I'll take care of it."

Someone knocks on Ernesto Wesley's front door. He says everything will be okay and pulls himself away from the conversation with the woman. He goes inside quickly. Everything will be okay is an expression that Ernesto Wesley uses with frequency. Practically every day he says it to someone.

***

Fire reproduces in fire, and what keeps it alive is oxygen, the same thing that keeps man alive. Without oxygen a fire will self-extinguish, and man too. Like man, fire needs to nourish itself to keep burning. It voraciously devours everything around. Suffocate a man, and he'll die because he's unable to breathe. Smother a flame, and it also dies.

Flames stay ablaze as they burn through wood, a mattress, or curtains, among other flammable products. Human beings are flammable products, too, that will keep a fire creeping for a long time. They survive on the same principle, and when they're facing off, they want to destroy each other, to devour one another. Since man discovered fire, he has tried to dominate it. But fire won't ever be dominated.

In general, overburdened electrical wires that, in turn, superheat domestic appliances are the cause of home fires. But, in this case, a thickset, full-breasted woman with coarse mustache and frizzled hair (insinuating a light dementia) living on the eighth floor was responsible for starting the fatal accident. She lit candles for Saint Anthony, protector of domestic animals, people with boils, and gravediggers. She prayed for her rheumatic pup, Ti-Ti, and went to take a bath. The heat source that ignited the fire was a fallen candle.

This eight-story building is sided with yellow ceramic tiles. The windows are armed with aluminum grid frames and granulated glass. The concrete structure is made up of apartment blocks, six per floor. All inhabited. Wind helps spread flames. The flames extend from some windows lapping at the building's façade. Fire is a kind of spectacle. Little Ernesto Wesley rarely had opportunities to see a spectacle. Entertainment was limited to children's games and some TV after dinner, but there were constant brownouts in the neighborhood. It was not uncommon for the family to gather together in one room enveloped by the oscillating glow of a handheld candle on a saucer. The large misshapen shadows on the wall began to seem like relatives. Electric light dispersed everyone, each to their own corner of the house. But candlelight united them and made them a family. When there was energy he missed the deformed shadows on the walls. When there were brownouts, the family spent hours talking and joking. And, he learned that candlelight arouses nostalgia and a kind of sheltering that was new to him. The illuminating glow welcomed and cherished him. Ernesto Wesley spent a good deal of time listening to stories wrapped in the family portrait of a delicately emblazoned and firm flame.

Fire can be fascinating, but it's an assassin. Faced with an incendiary, water's not always enough to put it out; scientific knowledge of its tricks is also necessary. When a sudden explosion occurs, air currents dislocate and modify fire's responses; sometimes it advances directly, sounding intentions, and bedeviling understanding. Fire can hide in invisible cracks, and will strike out on any airburst. Combustion in wood, paper, or plastic can be contained with water. If the origin is flammable liquid or electrical, carbon dioxide can be used. When fires propagate from flammable metals, like titanium, a chemical powder is indicated, such as sodium chloride, capable of creating a heavy crust on the flaming metal to insulate it from oxygen. Each fire is a specific type. In all forms, it's necessary to asphyxiate it by isolating it from oxygen; it's the only thing capable of extinguishing it. If it's not asphyxiated in time, the fire will asphyxiate us.

With the help of another firefighter, Ernesto Wesley finishes donning his fully protective gear and respiratory equipment. He grabs a flashlight and a portable radio, for communications with operation command. Total weight added: thirty-one kilos, making transpiration and respiration more difficult, and aggravating his physical and emotional stability. Generally, after climbing multiple flights of stairs, he returns with an unconscious body over his shoulder. Ernesto Wesley can bear two times his weight. But the repetition of excessive stress cannot be calculated. He's one of the few firefighters who can reach high-up places in the requisite time.

The fire has spread to the third floor. A team of firemen helps put out flames from outside with the aid of a mechanical ladder that reaches the top of the building. Another team enters the building to contain the fire on the inside and rescue victims. Ernesto Wesley adjusts his helmet, grabs an ax, and runs headlong into the building with the others.

A command post, established in the lobby of the building, controls communication with the fighters and provides operational details.

Firemen need to deal with the euphoria that comes to those witnessing a fire for the first time, and the despair of those whose relatives and friends are in the building.

Ernesto Wesley attempts to go in precisely where everyone else is trying to exit. He climbs the stairs quickly, keeping pace with his colleagues, until he reaches the eighth floor. The further up he goes, the more intense the heat and the black curtain of thick smoke he has to cross. Arriving on the eighth floor, he hears the cries of people still caught in their apartments. His hearing is sharp, and between the sputtering and the crackling of the fire, along with the heat that affects his thinking and all the weight bearing down on him, he still needs to distinguish the sounds around him. He breaks through the door of

Apartment 802 with his ax, and defends himself from the fire that advances on him. The flames are airborne and Ernesto runs through the fire to the back of the room. The heat takes its time to slowly suffocate him. His lungs are accustomed to it and his skin too. Ernest puts his arms around the naked woman curled in a corner. She's screaming that her father's in the bedroom. She calls for him; she insists they go in there. In the midst of fire, Ernesto is coldly calculating. He needs to rescue one at a time. He pays no heed to the woman's frantic clamor, because there exists an order to saving lives that mustn't be broken. The woman hits him, begs him to save her father. "He's crippled!" she yells. "He's in bed." He crosses to the other side of the room with her wrapped in his arms and deposits her with another fireman in the hallway for shelter. Ernesto Wesley moves along a somber, sooty corridor and kicks down a door. The room is enveloped in flames, only flames. He hears moaning. He advances to the end of the hall without visibility, surpassing his limits, airless, vertiginous. He crashes through the door with his ax and finds the man is lying in bed encircled by fire. The panicked old man screams and clings to the bed. He wraps the skinny, wrinkled man in a quilt and holds him in his arms. Ceiling plaster caves next to him. The fire has spread throughout the hall. Ernesto is trapped. So he walks through flames. He can sense them in his boots and heavy clothing. The flames advance like serpents. He carries the old man downstairs and exits the building. A first aid team places the old man on a gurney and Ernesto Wesley goes back inside the building. A report has someone stuck on the fifth floor, where the fire is most intense. The major preoccupation is that hydrogen cyanide gas has been released—burning foams and plastics produce a highly poisonous gas that can kill dozens in a matter of minutes. Having escaped flames, it's still possible to be trapped by smoke and instantaneously poisoned. Fire poisons air and kills. The flames' brightness gives it magnitude, a bewitching, destructive spectacle. On the fifth floor the fire hasn't been contained yet. Ernesto Wesley can't enter the smoke-filled apartments. By radio communication he receives confirmation that the floor's unoccupied and he's told to exit immediately; there's a high alert for collapse. Ernesto Wesley can't make his way down the stairs; the curtain of thick smoke has made visibility impossible. So he goes up to the seventh floor where the fire's controlled. He communicates with the command post by radio and they tell him to wait for new orders. They'll keep him informed about conditions on the lower floors. Floor and walls crackle. Ernesto enters an apartment and goes to a window with a view to the street to observe his buddies at work. The aerial apparatus is positioned at the fifth floor, and he can see that there's another team inside the building controlling the fire.

Ernesto Wesley walks amid the wreckage. He's used to it. What remains around him is aftermath. He props his ax against his left shoulder and walks along the hallway, intrigued. An inquiry is always necessary after putting out a fire, since fire dissimulates in places like interfacing, wall drafts, floorboards, elevator shafts, and telephone ducts. Ernesto is cautious. He pushes a door to one of the apartments open a crack with the tip of his finger and inspects the location. He scours every room. He finds a locked door. He knows from the baseboards that fire's been inside that room, and becomes suspicious of the door's temperature. He gets down on the ground but sees nothing by the narrow crack under the door. Ernesto Wesley could break through with his ax, but that's a move for a recruit. Fire's insidious.

"I need someone up here with the hose."

"We've cleared seven."

"I think you missed a detail."

"It's all under control."

"I'd like to speak to my team commander."

"I'm in command. You can come down, sergeant."

"Sir, I need a man here with a hose."

"My order is for you to leave the floor and come out."

"But something's wrong."

Radio interference keeps Ernesto Wesley from continuing.

He hangs out the window and signals to a colleague on his team. The man grabs a hose and walks into the building. The commander who gave the order to suspend operations blocks the firefighter. He radios someone on his team, and the firefighter, who's on one of the floors below him, quickly reaches the seventh floor.

"There's something here. The door's locked. They didn't check this room," says Ernesto Wesley.

The man with the hose positions himself beside the door for protection, while Ernesto Wesley raises his ax against the door; it cracks on the third swing. When the door finally breaks with a kick, the enfeebled fire swells and launches forcefully against Ernesto. The man with the hose manages the fire that's spreading rapidly through the room. Ernesto radios again to the command post and triggers the team into action. Three fighters are sent as backup. They manage to keep the flames from rekindling in the other rooms and, when everything's under control again, a tragic portrait appears of what seems to be two children and an adult in an embrace. The bodies are partially fused with metallic objects; gnarled, they create a new form.

Having dominated fire, Ernesto Wesley will now help account for the dead. Along with another firefighter, he carries corpses from the building.

It's a dreadful, almost superhuman job. The cooked bodies smell of sulfur, carrion, and smoke. After extinguishing the fire, the team gathers the bodies and lines them up on the sidewalk. In this operation, five people died and, due to the state of the corpses, teeth will be used for accurate identification. However, in cases like this, identification is more efficiently accomplished since each corpse was found in a given apartment.

An hour later the fire is dampened on all floors. All that's left are slender foci of smoke.

Ernesto Wesley climbs onto a fire truck already in motion to leave. His shift's ended and it's time to return to headquarters.

He sits between two firemen and they bounce around in silence, since the sirens are off.

One of the firemen shakes his head in denial as he vaguely stares at his own boots. He has an oblique, numb expression. He mutters a few words and gradually raises his voice.

"A candle for Saint Tony. My mother prayed to him when I had boils," he says. "Sometimes one can't even pray."

The soot covering each man makes them slightly sinister in appearance. The grief contained in the firefighter's voice is plaintive and pained.

"Sometimes all one *can* do is pray," says Ernesto Wesley.

"How did you know there were bodies in that room?" asks another fireman.

Ernesto Wesley takes a deep breath. He's tired, the orbits of his eyes are red and his hoarse voice doesn't seem to belong to him.

"Having worked at this for a while, I can smell a burned body kilometers away," responds Ernesto.

"That's true," says another fireman who's been quiet so far. "Ernesto can tell who each dirty sock in the firehouse belongs to by its odor. He's got the best nose I know."

The man laughs.

"Is it why you decided to be a firefighter?"

Ernesto Wesley sighs and rubs his eyes. He's very tired.

"No. I became a firefighter because I had the courage to go where no one else would," responds Ernesto Wesley.

The men, dumbstruck, reflect momentarily before nodding. The truck enters the firehouse garage and Ernesto Wesley gets down and walks directly to the locker room. Naked, he checks his own body. Apparently he's okay. He puts ointment on places he finds burns, especially his hands and feet. He steps out onto the firehouse patio to smoke a cigarette. It's a chilly dawn, with partially cloudy skies; a sliver of an opaque moon struggles to remain fixed between the stars.

CHAPTER 4

The planet is finite and transitory. As the space to store trash dwindles, so too does the space to inhume bodies. Some decades or centuries from now there'll be more bodies beneath the earth than on it. We'll be stepping on our ancestors, neighbors, relatives, and enemies, like we step on dry grass: without even noticing it. Ground soil and water will be contaminated with leachate, liquid containing toxic substances that drains from bodies in decomposition. Death has the power to generate death. And it spreads, even if mostly unperceived.

In spite of a certain melancholy that comes over him when he thinks of the incinerated, Ronivon knows that asepsis is best achieved by setting mortal remains on fire. Otherwise to think of the end of the world is to think of mountains of dross and the earth soaked through with the inhumed.

He raises the collar on his coat and rubs his hands together. He stares out the window fifty centimeters above grass level onto the garden and notices a thin fog. Winter this year will be the hardest in thirty years, and he hopes the furnaces will work and emit as much heat as possible. He takes the still sealed letter he'd left on the table for Ernesto Wesley, out of his pocket. Days have passed and neither he nor Ernesto has opened it. In a few days they'll receive another, and a few days later another, and so on, he imagines.

The door to the retort room opens and Palmiro enters slowly, grumbling about the rheumatism that bothers him on cold days. He's wearing two pairs of pants, three jackets, and this extra weight makes walking considerably more difficult. He carries a thermos of fresh coffee and some disposable cups. Ronivon places the envelope back in his pocket, grabs a cup, and pours himself some hot coffee.

"Today I woke with pain all over," says Palmiro.

"You need to take care."

"I need to retire. I'm old, tired, and sick. But this place is all I have. If I leave, I'd become a vagrant."

"What about your daughter? Have you managed to speak to her?"

"No. I wrote two weeks ago, and she still hasn't responded."

"When was the last time you two spoke?"

"I think it's been eight years," sighs the tired man.

Ronivon gulps down some more coffee and contemplates the day through the fifty-centimeters of visibility.

"What's the flow like today?"

"Medium. I don't think it'll be too much work."

"Wednesdays are like this, aren't they? Less work. Fewer corpses to cremate," comments Ronivon, warming his hands on his cup.

"Yes, seems like it. Death finds other days more favorable."

Ronivon agrees, gently nods. He extends the cup in his hand for Palmiro to pour more coffee.

"I think I'll take J.G. home with me. The new janitor will be staying in his room," says Ronivon.

"You're doing a good thing. J.G. needs friends. Poor guy spends his life in this place and then will be buried under one of the rosebushes he planted and cares for himself."

Ronivon smiles. Thinking of it makes him feel better somehow.

"I think J.G. dreams of just that. He loves this place, the guavas, and the roses."

"But he's scared shitless of the dead," Palmiro says, laughing.

They remain quiet for a few moments. Palmiro dries his blind eye, which is tearing. Palmiro could share his room at the back of the crematorium with J.G., if there were space. The room is spare: it has a single bed with a two-door built-in dresser and a two-burner stove, a grimy sink, and an old buffet, with a twenty-inch television on it. The television is new. Palmiro paid 400 reais for it over ten installments without interest. J.G. lives in a similarly laid-out room next door, and they share a bath, and a fridge that's installed in the "warehouse," the narrow storage space between the two rooms. The old janitor didn't live at the crematorium, so J.G. could use his little room. Palmiro will really miss J. G., and the stupid conversations they have. He's like a good dog that can stay hours at his side in silence. He never complains. Always satisfied, with a small smile on his lips in case anyone looks at him for more than five seconds. He's loyal and a good companion. On weekends, it's common for them to sit on a bench, side by side, wordlessly observing the well-cut lawn in the expansive gardens. Palmiro usually carries a transistor radio and a bottle of cachaça on these days off. They're simple men, with no apparent anxieties, and they carry their burdens quietly.

"I'm hoping for the same for me. I'd like to rest my ashes beneath a guava tree—that one, by the entrance over there. Remember that, Ronivon."

Palmiro opens his mouth, pulls his lips apart with his fingers, and displays eight golden crowns to Ronivon.

"And don't forget to remove these, okay? And send them to my daughter. They're worth a good sum. Always will be. Every investment I ever made in life is in my mouth. No one will rob me, no one can repossess it, no pressure from the bank. No worries. The gold stays here in my wilted mouth embalmed in my *pinga* breath."

Palmiro laughs deeply and then coughs. He coughs continuously until he coughs phlegm into a handkerchief. He turns around and opens the door leading to the hall and moves along it to the stairs.

Ronivon returns his attention to the retort and evaluates its temperature. Everything's working well. His eyes rest on the wall clock and he notes this cremation will be done in thirty minutes. Geverson, the grinder, responsible for pulverizing cremains, comes out of the little room where he works. He takes off his gloves and protective eyewear.

"I finished two more," says Geverson. "It's so cold in there, they're cooling off quickly."

"Palmiro just came by with fresh coffee," says Ronivon.

"I'll take a break to warm up a little too."

"He was just here with the thermos."

Geverson removes a small piece of metal from his pocket. He holds the object up to the little window, between index finger and thumb, and attentively observes it in the filtered daylight.

"I found this when I passed my magnet over the ashes."

"Whose ashes?"

"The man's," he mutters, focused.

Ronivon gets the clipboard off the desk and checks for the dead man's name.

"Mr. Anibal. Yep, must be his."

"This was inside him."

"Let me take a look."

Ronivon checks the little object and is reminded that he didn't detect any metal on the body of the dead man when he passed the metal detector over him.

"Do you suppose it was in his teeth?" asks Geverson.

"Maybe."

"Uh huh . . . we never really know. What does it matter, right?" says Geverson shrugging his shoulders and turning his back.

It's not uncommon for incinerated bodies to reveal fragments when grinding their ashes, and the men don't ever discover what they're from.

Geverson takes the object back and puts it in a can on the table containing a handful of other small non-identified metal objects.

Geverson takes off his apron and hangs it behind the door.

He pats some dust off his body and cracks his fingers. He stretches big and yawns.

"This year's going to be the worst winter in thirty years," he comments.

"Yes, I read about it," says Ronivon.

They stand side by side silently contemplating the frigid day through their fifty-centimeter window view.

"Want some coffee?"

"I've got acid reflux. I'm cold and my stomach burns like an inferno."

Geverson presses on his belly button and moans. The two men continue contemplating the frigid day through the window.

"Try to get some warm milk from Nadine."

"Good idea. I'll see if I can arrange that."

Ronivon checks the temperature gauge. Through the viewport on the retort chamber he verifies that everything's going perfectly. Back in front of the window he takes another, last sip of coffee. He'd like a little more, but Palmiro's next round is in two hours.

"Tomorrow they'll do maintenance on the furnaces," says Ronivon.

"The cremulator also needs to be checked. It's becoming difficult to grind with it like this."

"No shifts in the morning."

"Where'd you see that?"

"Reception. It's on the bulletin board."

"I never notice these things."

Palmiro opens the door, thermos in hand.

"There's some coffee left over. I came by to see if you wanted more."

Ronivon holds out his cup and Geverson gets one for himself. As they serve themselves, they comment on how cold the day is.

"Tomorrow they're doing maintenance, right, Palmiro?" asks Geverson.

"Yes. They'll do maintenance on the thermoelectric converter as well. They're expecting it'll be very cold this year and they'll turn on the heaters," says Palmiro.

"Let's hope there are enough corpses to generate energy for it," says Ronivon. "If not, things'll get tough around here."

"The dead are reliable," says Geverson.

The others nod in agreement.

"There shouldn't be any problem. Boss is negotiating for the victims of a large accident. All burnt," says Palmiro.

"Airplane accident?" asks Geverson.

"Looks like it," says Palmiro.

"I hadn't heard," responds Geverson.

"I heard something about it on the radio," says Ronivon.

"Well, if this load arrives we'll have enough heat," concludes Palmiro, leaving.

Ronivon and Geverson have some more coffee and admire the lackluster day outside.

"The day's quite beautiful, even overcast," sighs Geverson.

"Sometimes it's better like this. Overcast," adds Ronivon.

Geverson nods. The two men stand there, admiring the overcast, low-visibility day, waiting on a load of corpses to guarantee the heat and energy necessary for the living to go on living.

CHAPTER 5

The heat generated by the crematory furnaces passes through a circuit connected to a thermoelectric converter that transforms heat into electric energy. The heat of cremation offsets a portion of the energy used at the crematorium and at the hospital, a kilometer away, and some of the other commercial establishments in the area too. The hospital sends its dead, especially the indigents, for cremation at Colina dos Anjos, and their heat is transformed into energy to power the living. The residents living in Abalurdes know how to make use of their dead.

The coffee machines in the cafeteria, the sacred music that plays in the chapels, all the bulbs in the garden lampposts, the computers, and the cremulator are driven on energy produced from the heat of the charnel furnaces. This energy produced by the converter is vital for the operation of the hospital, which attends people living in a 150 kilometers radius. Hospital deaths are vital to the operation of the crematory retorts and, consequently, for generating energy for the converter.

The electricity shortage began five years ago. Across the region charcoal factories and mines supply most of the population's energy needs. Using char generated by burning the dead is still a segregated experiment, but a practice that will become common in years to come. Cities are in collapse. Soil is soaked through with the inhumed. Fire in its brute state has become a primary source of power. It's as if the clock's turned back to primitive times. Distant, isolated areas were the first to experience scarcity. As the years pass, it'll affect everyone. The

Abalurdes region is on the verge of discoveries, and holds sway in the imaginarium of some visionaries.

Abalurdes is a city nestled in a steep cliff face. The river is dead and mirrors the color of the sun. There are no fish in the contaminated waters. The sky, even clear, turns ashen in the evenings. It's muddy and cold on winter days. On the outskirts of town, houses are a faded, simple brick. Roads are treacherous in some of the far-flung areas, with mere vestiges of ancient asphalt. The main thoroughfare is badly illuminated and absent of traffic lights, and there are many sharp curves bordering the long cliffs.

Abalurdes is a carboniferous region. It has a railroad for the region's mineral coal extraction. Exploration began fifty years ago and thousands of tons of mineral coal continue to be mined.

The local men return home from the coalfields unrecognizable, coated in dense soot. A thin layer of dust clings to all surfaces everywhere. Some live in a mining camp near the pit.

The coal wash is still done in the rivers and over the years the waters have turned an orange hue from the oxidation of iron in the Pyrite, a fool's gold extracted from the mines jointly with the coal. Most of the soil is unproductive, visibly dried out and colorless. Potable water for human consumption is scarce, and more than half the population has become affected by pulmonary dysfunction. Black lung disease is randomly liquidating adult miners and pit apprentices alike, beaten down, withered men, whose serrated skin is the worse for wear.

Men plunge into viscid gloom beneath graves, inhaling coal dust, obscured from the light of day. Accidents in the mines are common and many are buried alive. Not everyone has the intrepidness to work the coalfields. When they realize the pit depths, the total privation of sunlight, and high risk of premature burial, they desist. To reach these depths of darkness one must be courageous and willing to go where no one wants to go.

But there'll always be some hero with the heart to go anywhere. Edgar Wilson, at twenty-three, is one of the youngest apprentices in a colliery employing 113 men. He's hacked and shoveled coal since he was twenty, without vacation, with only two days "off" a year. And he's never suffered any serious injury. He uses shorts and an old pair of leather boots. He puts on a crash helmet, ties a battery lamp to his belt, and picks up his digger. He moves in the direction of the cage, his colleagues follow. Edgar Wilson's workday is about to begin. He lives a kilometer from the coalfield in the mining camp with the other men. His pale skin is begrimed. Edgar Wilson's got a yellowish hue, and there's soot in his spit and mud in his eyes. Gray is the color of his gaze after uncountable hours 200-meters deep inhaling toxic fumes, deprived of sun and sky. The day he leaves this job he's determined to contemplate the sky for the rest of the time he has on Earth.

The two men—each carrying a water bottle, a coffee thermos, and their respective lunchboxes wrapped in muddy dish towels—enter the iron cage; the kind of apparatus used in constructions: two platforms, one above the other, each with a capacity for six men. They fill the hold to the maximum with miners, and one works the winding gear. It takes four minutes to drop to a depth of 200 meters. Stitches of natural light evaporate in the first twenty seconds. Thereafter, it's a place mute of all light. That's when Edgar Wilson relies on his yellow and hesitant lamp. As the apparatus drops into the void, it acquires an echo like a distorted howl.

The darkness of a coalfield is humid. It'll start dripping, raining little pieces, indication that it's taking weight and stuff and might collapse. This blind world compresses the senses. Makes it difficult to breathe. Little by little these men become a part of it; concealed in the toxic shadows of noxious smoke. Outside the mine, Edgar Wilson likes to light up. He's come to like the taste of soot, burn, and fire. He learned to smoke with the other men in the mining camp. Some men even smoke in the pit. It's impossible to control everyone. It's difficult to deal with hired men. They're brutish, characteristically primitive, and hardly obedient. Dealing with temporary workers is like pasturing donkeys in the desert. The location of a coalfield is a kind of desert. Isolated, sweltering, abundantly dusty, and lonely, even among so many coal miners. The extensive proportions of Earth all around can squelch the human condition, even as it appears in the most brutal of men. Like asses, they're impossible to dominate. Rebellious, they'll throw anyone who tries to mount them, and when they have, they'll step on them and even try to bite them. Bestial in so many ways: these men and asses.

The man who got into the apparatus next to Edgar Wilson is called Rui. He's been working in the coalfields for twenty years. He's twice as old as Edgar Wilson and has no other skill besides this one. Rui intends to dig mineral carbon as long as he lives. The black fossil-color of his skin also runs in his blood. He suffers from black lung disease, but the ailment hasn't kept him yet from work. He constantly coughs and spits up viscid black sputum. He intends to finish out his days here, in the pit, because all his life, all he's ever done is work. He doesn't have a clue how to do anything else, not even how to make babies. Like Edgar, he's living in the company mining camps with fifty other men. Still others go home to their families. The majority visits home only two or three times a year, because of the distances. They're on the job for twelve hours. Edgar drops into the pit at 5:30 in the morning and returns to the surface at 5:30 in the evening. They snatch a quarter of an hour or so to eat the food they've brought with them in one of the galleries. For three years this man has known only first light and evening dusk. Occasionally when there's quiet in the mining camp, he tries to recall the color of day, the clarity of sun and its heat.

They're downward hurled in silence. His entire body projects into the Earth, and is engrailed in its dimensions of darkness. Rui chews on his tongue, and foams the saliva accumulated in the corner of his mouth. These deep dimensions of the Earth amplify sounds and sensations. The apparatus drops through a narrow haulage way, and it's possible to touch the walls of the long shaft as it passes. The wooden props holding up the beams and girders tend to buckle from the water pressure pushing in from all sides.

After a two-minute run, Rui crawls out into one of the galleries and lets out a yelp, he's heading into battle. He follows along a dark mucky corridor in his roughed up cowboy boots, printed shirt, and faded jeans.

Edgar Wilson continues to the pit bottom. He inspects the walls just a few centimeters from his face. They're rustic excavations. The only thing he truly fears is his lamp battery dying. Complete blackness at the center of the Earth horrifies him. He wouldn't know how to egress. He wouldn't know where to find the shaft exit. The deeper he goes, the more he thinks of his worms, but his thoughts are tepid at such depths. Worms are meant for humidity and darkness. Man is not. That must be why so many get sick. The apparatus stops and he crawls off. Now, he needs to head into the core of the mine. Two kilometers by way of a flooded labyrinth. Four other men wait for him there. Edgar Wilson settles into a tub jolting slowly inward, pulled by a small tractor. It rattles along a straight line, creeping toward deeper workings and the coalface where the men are discussing the previous day's soccer match amid laughter and laments.

***

After hacking and shoveling the coalface without pause for three hours, Edgar Wilson stops to drink water. In the gallery, the men's work has already rendered two tub-loads of coal, which are pulled along the rails by two men assigned to the task. The interminable sound of picks hacking at coal. Every night when all is silent around him, he still hears it. Suddenly, in mere seconds, Edgar Wilson eternalizes a strange sensation. A foreboding makes him glance over his shoulder. A slight air current crosses his back, very slight yet perceptible to his acute senses. The darkness thickens. When excavating mineral carbon, a colorless gas made up of methane is sometimes released. Inhaling it won't cause dizziness or any other symptoms, but it's combustive when accumulated in large quantities. A simple spark from a lamp can ignite an explosion. The mine exhausts have been off for two days due to an electrical shortage, and were to begin again at the end of the afternoon. It was a fierce blast that hurled men distances of ten or twelve meters and sent the girders into collapse. In addition to being poisonous, combustive gas incinerates, and kills by asphyxiation. Edgar Wilson keeps his eyes open, but is blinded by the extreme darkness. His lamp disappeared when he was hurled to the depths of the Earth like a dweller of subterranean faults. Without a lamp beam, he pulls himself out of the great puddle of water and mud into which he's been thrown. His fall into the puddle prevented him from incinerating. He painfully gropes his way along the walls. He's not badly bruised, and that's all. He hears cries for help, suffocated moans, and for the first time in his life, he panics. He tries to guide himself by the sound of dripping. The smoke is thick and solid as a block of concrete. He takes off his shirt, dips it in the puddle and ties it around his face as a kind of filter, so he can breathe.

It's impossible to think of looking for someone in these circumstances, he needs to find a shaft exit and go for help. He thinks of all the men working down there with him. He clutches the charm around his neck and mutters a prayer. He puts his head down and runs through the fog of dust. He gasps for air, and his head throbs. Edgar is advancing but feels pain in his chest. His thighs are stiff, and he trips over heavy legs. He continues to pray while traveling the tenuous path, groping at the ruined boarding and roof. He continues blindly not knowing where to find the tunnel exit. At the main entrance, other men expect to be rescued. They huddle on the ground in fear and patiently wait. Edgar Wilson shuts his eyes and pictures a blue sky. If he dies, this will be the memory imprinted on his mind. If he escapes alive, he'll never go into the entrails of the Earth again, but will work in daylight. He'll never again stay away from the sun.

A sliver of light beams through the darkness. Javêncio, the team leader, calls out to any man who may be still alive. The men yell back, and with that faint glimmer from Javêncio's torch, a group of twenty-three men manages to escape the sepulcher. They're taken up in the apparatus, untouched by the explosion, that returns them to the Earth's surface.

***

In the distance, the lunar landscape's got a desolate quality, overmastered by motionless mountains of black coal and smokestacks that still, after many long hours, suffocate remaining vestiges of hope. Ernesto Wesley has been here for eight hours. The first team of firefighters didn't waste any time getting to the incident. However, when they arrived the high concentrations of carbonic gas from the burning oils, wood, and the coal itself, led them to fear there could be additional explosions, and they anxiously sat on their hands for hours. This is the heaviest and riskiest trial of Ernesto Wesley's career. A smell of charcoal, both mineral and human, wafts from the pithead. The bodies, more than fifty, are piled in the order they were extracted, and most are unrecognizable. Ernesto Wesley draws on more courage than he's ever before needed to now enter the center of the burning Earth, 200-meters deep. He's reassured that there's nothing he can't do, and there's no limit to his Atlantes-like boldness. Or that of his colleagues. He's filthy. The soot, the smoke, and noxious odor of toxic pollutants, the devastation, and the heat of the fire mixes with the cold of the day to squash these men, but they continue advancing into the shadows, carrying out dead bodies with anguished expressions. Many are twisted and mutilated. Fingers torn and sometimes severed, as if they'd been dragging themselves in search of air. Death by suffocation is slow and causes desperation. The chest collapses over time and the victim suffers gradually. It's an anguished death. After eight hours of work Ernesto Wesley has been authorized to rest.

He takes off his helmet and washes his face and rinses out his mouth with water he pours from a bottle. He drinks the rest and dries his face on a piece of cloth from the truck. He fills a disposable cup with coffee brought by a lady who's been trying to encourage the men since the beginning of the accident. Though, like most of the people in the region she's obviously poor, she brings them cake and coffee. She's not the kind of woman to remain inert in the face of another's troubles. She's the rare woman who by goodness makes cake and coffee appear and multiply, and thus eases their journey into the abyss.

"By the looks of it, you still have a lot of work ahead," comments the woman.

"Yes, ma'am," says Ernesto Wesley.

"This was bound to happen. Everybody knows how dangerous the gases are down there. Thank God my son Douglas got laid off last week, or he'd have been here too. I've already given so many thanks—I came here to help others best I could—God spared my son."

Some men approach the woman for cake and coffee, and she begins to tell them the same story she just finished telling him.

Ernesto Wesley sits a few meters from the pithead hoping to breathe less contaminated black air. He combs his hair and lights a cigarette. He sips his coffee slowly. He's got a twenty-minute break and he's learned to appreciate this short period without rushing. Soot sits heavy on his lashes. He looks with emotion at the pile of human charcoal next to the pile of mineral charcoal. It's impossible to know which is blacker. If mixed, men and fossil would blend.

Crouching next to a puddle, Edgar Wilson spits up dark bile. His gaze is fixed on the horizon and his face is unruffled. Behind the crust of carbon that covers his skin, hiding his fair complexion and chestnut hair, he seems unshakeable. Ernesto Wesley looks at him but doesn't move.

"Yo, man!" says Ernesto Wesley.

No response.

"Yo, man . . . were you down there?"

Edgar remains quiet. Ernesto Wesley repeats himself, and Edgar Wilson unlocks his gaze and attention from that immutable point that held him silent.

"Yes?" Edgar Wilson reacts.

"Were you down there? In the mine?" asks Ernesto Wesley.

Edgar takes a moment to respond by nodding.

"Are you all right? What's your name? Feeling okay, man?" insists Ernesto.

"I think so," says Edgar.

Ernesto Wesley gets up and moves in to take a closer look because where he's sitting smoke's in his eyes.

"Hey, man, how are you? You should get yourself to the hospital."

"I'm okay," Edgar Wilson sighs, "I'm really okay."

Edgar rubs his red eyes.

"You don't look okay to me."

"I don't know how a person should look when they've just escaped death, but this is the face I've got, sir."

Ernesto takes a sip of his now lukewarm coffee. A fine mist deposits a delicate layer of dew over the men.

"See those bodies? I dragged a bunch of them to the mouth of the tunnel. When I reached the tunnel's entrance, I found other men waiting for help, screaming . . . everyone thought they were going to die."

Edgar Wilson spits on the ground, his lungs are impregnated with the charcoal dust. He coughs.

"Then Javêncio, the team leader, appeared with his lamp to lead us out of there. He had another flashlight with him. The others went with him, but I took the lamp and went to find my buddies who stayed behind in the dark."

Edgar Wilson pauses. He looks at the sky. It's a cloudy day, no sign of sun, but still some daylight. This comforts him.

"I was able to bring ten men out to the exit. I repeated the trip so many times I didn't need the lamp anymore. I was a goddamn bat," he chuckles, and then turns bitter.

"I lifted them one-by-one on my back. Two were still alive: Everaldo and Rui. Everaldo's going to be married next week and we've been planning a party for him. Rui's an older guy, worked the mines his whole life. Rui was dying down there, and asked me to stay with him. Said he didn't want to be carried out, he'd rather be buried in the mine, so I obeyed, because I always obey Rui. He knows things. I pulled him into a gallery and squeezed him inside a narrow crawlspace that opened up during the explosion, and I covered him with shale. When I returned, Everaldo had died. We won't be having a party here now."

Ernesto Wesley listens in silence. He lowers his eyes, respectfully. He understands perfectly, and knows this miner will never forget what happened here. He hopes it makes him better at everything, because this experience will influence his character and strengthen his spirit. Edgar Wilson threatens to leave.

"Where are you headed?" asks Ernesto Wesley.

"I'm leaving. I have nothing left here."

"You should stay and give testimony. You were down there and you survived."

"I have nothing left here."

"And what will you do, man?"

"I'm going to take a job offered to me some time ago. If it's still open."

"Are you sure you'll be okay?"

"I think so."

"What'll you do?"

"I'll slaughter pigs. And never take my eyes off the open sky again."

Edgar Wilson moves in the direction of the mining camp, where he picks up his belongings and whatever money he was able to save. He never lost sight of the sun after that.

CHAPTER 6

After several months of work, Ernesto Wesley was up for promotion, and if all continued smoothly he'd get it. For a year he'd been working twice weekly at the Colina dos Anjos crematorium, at the coal-maker reserved for indigents and animals. He was in debt, surviving on a very small salary. At a party at his house, he dressed for the first time in a fireman's uniform. Things are going to fall into place now, he thought as he ate a slice of cake with frosting, made by his wife, sharing it with his four-year-old daughter.

On his daughter's fifth birthday, he traded the nightshift for the day to help his wife out with the little party she was preparing for their daughter. His wife also found someone to cover for her so that she could leave work early. She worked as a cashier in a supermarket two kilometers from home.

Vladimilson, Ernesto Wesley and Ronivon's older brother, stopped by the house to pick up his niece to whom he'd promised a birthday present. The babysitter, a fifteen-year-old neighbor, didn't want to let the girl go with her uncle without the parents' permission. She tried calling them from a public phone but couldn't reach them. Rosilene felt a tightening where the esophagus meets the stomach when she saw Vladimilson put the child in the car. She insisted on going with them, but he refused. Said he'd be back soon, they were going into town to buy a present. Rosilene tried calling Ernesto a few more times, since he was at the station and it's generally easier to reach him than the girl's mother, but the line was busy. Insistently busy.

Rosilene went back inside the house, upset. There was nothing more she could do. She decided to wash some of the girl's clothes and to finish making lunch: spaghetti with ground beef and tomato sauce. She hung the clothes on the line. It was a sunny day and the breeze would dry the clothes quickly. Two pots on the stove: spaghetti boiling in one, and ground beef, tomato extract, and parsley pan-frying in the other. Rosilene sat down at the kitchen table and, although she was hungry, she couldn't eat. The qualm in her belly hadn't passed.

From the kitchen table she could see the clothes swinging on the line. They were secured by clothespins. It was windy. She was enveloped by the smell of food, clothes balancing on the line, and silence. She sat there. She was just sitting, quietly, when a tear dropped on the table. She'd been crying without knowing it. She dabbed the corners of her eyes. She looked at the clothes on the line as they gradually stopped swinging, and for some minutes nothing moved. The wind had passed. Rosilene went out into the yard, and all was still. Eternalized. She looked back at the clothes, swinging again now on a new gust of wind. She went to the front of the house, sat down on the sidewalk and waited.

Rosilene's mother was the first to arrive. She was wearing a cotton dress, a dirty apron, and, in her hands, she carried a dish-cloth. She walked deliberately, measuring her steps. It signaled bad news when she walked like this. The news came first to the phone of the greengrocer by their house. Rosilene hugged her even before her mother told her what had happened.

That stretch of road was known as "the curve in the devil's spine." Others called it demon's lordosis. After hitting a worn out concrete barrier on the side of the road, the car flipped three times. The girl was in the back seat, holding onto the doll she'd received from her uncle. He recalled that she screamed twice as soon as they hit, and then a sort of muted echo filled his ears. The first thing he saw, when he opened his eyes, was the face of a young man asking if he was all right. Vladimilson felt the impact of the accident, but was okay. The door on the driver's side was jammed and other men who appeared tried to force it open. He looked behind and saw the girl's arm crushed in a tangle of metal. He called for her. She was still alive when the firemen showed up. Vladimilson managed to crawl out of the car when they pulled off the door, and was standing, with a few cuts on his face and chest, when Ernesto Wesley arrived to help them. Ernesto Wesley never liked using the metal cutting saw, and on that day he was spared. When they removed his little girl, she was dead. He died there then too.

Vladimilson was arrested, since levels of intoxication were detected. Ernesto Wesley never again spoke to his brother, who was condemned to eight years of prison.

Ernesto Wesley's wife began to languish after their daughter's death. She took time off and sat for hours in a plastic lawn chair, forgotten together in the yard. Thus, months passed. Ernesto Wesley became quieter and gloomier. One night, he came home from work to find his wife passed out on the living room floor. He sat next to her and hugged her tenderly for an hour. She was already dead. She'd taken an excess of pills. He didn't lose his composure for a minute.

He cremated the rest of his family the following day and buried his wife's ashes next to his daughter's at the base of a rosebush in the Colina dos Anjos reflective gardens.

He took two months off, during which time no one had any news of him. But he returned to work and seemed to be doing well. He never said where he'd been, and when they asked, said they shouldn't ask.

He rented a new house and invited his brother, Ronivon, to live with him. The two painted the walls and made repairs to the old house as needed, from plumbing to wiring. They managed to knock off three months' rent for the improvements to the property. After some months in the new house, Ernesto Wesley found Jocasta, abandoned at the door of a neighborhood grocer, in a cardboard box. He'd gone out early to buy the paper, it was

Saturday, his day off. He took the bitch home, carefully holding her in the palm of his hand. He fed her milk from a bottle and watched her grow. After a few weeks, he chose a name for her. Jocasta is an antidote for poison. She's the only woman of the house, he often says.

It's been two weeks since, at Ronivon's invitation, J.G. moved into the little room next to the kitchen. Jocasta is still wary of him, and J.G. is so leery of the worms, he can't so much as look at them. He decided to plant rosebushes in an empty area of the yard. Jocasta dug up their planting holes during the night and dragged the bushes here and there. That's the way it is now that J.G. moved in.

"Don't mind her, J.G., Jocasta will get used to you soon. She's practically the owner of the yard, but she's clever and knows who to obey," said Ernesto Wesley.

"She's a good dog, right Ernesto?" says J.G. finishing his breakfast.

"Yes. She's a good dog."

"I really want her to like me. But she doesn't. She doesn't like roses either."

"It'll be okay," said Ernesto rising from his chair.

A clap of hands at the back of the yard calls their attention. Ronivon goes to hear what Dona Zema, the neighbor with the hens, has to say. Dona Zema has a beheaded chicken in her hand; it's been eviscerated.

"Ronivon, days ago I spoke with Ernesto and he hasn't done a thing about that dog. Look at this! That dog is killing all my hens."

"Dona Zema, I . . ."

"Don't bother to ask me to stay calm. I want to know—what are you going to do about this?"

"We'll try to fix the fence."

"These hens are everything I have of value in life. The house isn't even mine—it belongs to my brother. I'm worth the price of my hens."

"Yes, ma'am, Dona Zema. The problem is the worms. Your chickens jump the fence to dig in our worm farm, and Jocasta won't let anyone—besides Ernesto and me—near those worms."

"Now, Ronivon, let me tell you something. That dog's got it coming, if you don't do something. If one more of my hens shows up with so much as a scratch that dog's got it coming," and with that threat, Dona Zema turns on her heels and returns to her chicken coop.

Ronivon enters the house, preoccupied.

"Ernesto, the woman's crazy mad. She threatened Jocasta," says Ronivon.

"I'll reinforce the fence as soon as I can."

"I once had a dog," says J.G. "but she was poisoned and when she died her tongue was hanging out."

"Dona Zema could do something bad to Jocasta," says Ronivon.

"I'll take care of it. Don't worry."

"Oh, and before I forget—Palmiro wants some dehydrated worms."

"I've got some in a can, I think."

Ernesto Wesley checks the can's contents and weighs it on a scale next to the sink.

"That's five reais. Tell him, later I'll send more. Is he making meal?"

"Yes, he's been grinding the worms and sprinkling them on his breakfast. He complains less about aches and pains."

"I like Palmiro's worm meal too. He always shares some with me," comments J.G.

Ronivon and J.G. put on their coats and scarves before heading out. It's a ten-minute walk to the bus stop, where they'll catch a bus to the crematorium. The last few days have been brutally cold. The coal-like aspect of the sky has intensified. The impossibility for sunrays to cut through the coal dust cover or the heavy storm clouds, gives Abalurdes a desolate aspect. An ashen desert, of sorts, nimbus clouds bearing down like concrete blocks. A dimensionless sky. In any direction as far as the eye can see, the sky is infinite, its disconsolate vastitude extends to the outermost limits of every citizen's perception.

The new janitor had been working as a gravedigger for thirty years at a neighboring city's cemetery. His name is Aparício and one of his legs is shorter than the other. When he was young, he stepped on bamboo and it stuck in his foot, but his father wouldn't take him to the hospital. He said he'd recover at home with herbal baths and compresses. His foot was crippled and when he was able to walk again with crutches, months later, the world took on a special undulation due to his movements. He didn't feel sure-footed and his crippled clod hung useless for years. His arms therefore became toned and firm, and he could dig seven palms at a considerable pace. To be a gravedigger was his lifelong ambition. He'd buried more than twenty-five relatives and acquaintances. When his father died, he dug a deeper hole. He gave it an extra palm. The extra depth was for years of ignorance and stupidity on the part of his father, a cruel and uncouth man with the family, and a good guy with the neighbors. False and underhanded. He had lovers and enjoyed humiliating the man who worked under him at the little market stand he was proud to say was his; a business he directed with a firm hand. It wasn't unusual for him to make fun of his son's crippled clod, and this made Aparício's hatred for his father mature. After burying him at eight palms, he felt distinct relief. He was advised to operate, and recovered fifty percent mobility in his foot. After months of physiotherapy, he started to wear an orthopedic shoe on the operated foot with an eight-centimeter lift in the heel. He finds it ironic that he should be raised eight centimeters while his father was lowered to a depth of eight palms. He still walks with difficulty, but the undulations have diminished by eight degrees, or so it seems to him.

Aparício's a good man. Burying his wife precipitated his move to Abalurdes. He's been a widower for a year and doesn't plan to marry again. His kids live in another city and all are married. He's a peaceful man who's seen the tears, desperation, and regrets of others nearly every day of his life. Though he takes Sundays off, and Christmas, he digs graves on all other days. In his career, he's buried some thirty-five thousand bodies. Corpses of all sorts. He likes to smoke a pipe and makes his own tobacco, something he learned from his grandfather. It's an aromatic tobacco that leaves a taste of mint lingering in his mouth. He smells of burnt herbs and his shirts are speckled with tiny holes where sparks fly from his pipe. Aparício inspires confidence and he's kindly to everyone.

After he rises and has breakfast in his small room that smells of dried urine, Aparício walks the border of the columbarium. He likes gardens, and this one at Colina dos Anjos is special and well kempt. A mist cover due to the morning frost makes distance-seeing difficult. Warmly bundled and wearing a wool hat, he raises the collar on his coat and walks habitually. He notices a dark and static blotch in the fog toward the middle of the garden, a few meters away. He avoids walking on the grass or on the dead, as that's how he considers it. Respect for the dead was a fear, one of the first, he acquired early on. The cold seals the morning with spectral whiteness. He steps onto the grass to inspect the blotch.

The blotch is Palmiro seated on a bench. The battery-powered radio in his coat pocket is still playing. At his feet, a bottle of the unlabeled pinga he's always drinking. Every week, he bought the same cachaça from a distillery at the outskirts of Abalurdes.

His lips are purple, and his expression is plastered to his face, rigor mortis appears to have set in. Aparício doesn't touch a thing. He places his index finger beneath the nose, but there's no sign of breath. Like all the plaster monuments erected around the memorial gardens, he's immobile.

No one has arrived yet. He makes a collect call to the manager on a public phone outside the crematorium. The man doesn't hesitate to come out.

It's a day of mourning in a place of mourning. Ronivon looks at the sack of dehydrated worms and puts them back in his backpack. J.G. stands silently and sadly still.

Palmiro died of a heart attack the previous night. It was very cold out and it was customary for him to sit on that bench listening to the radio and drinking. He was past drunk when he started to feel badly, too drunk to go for help.

After being released by the authorities, Palmiro's body was placed in the crematorium cooler, where it remained for two days. As he had no relatives to claim it, all that was left was to cremate his body and bury him at the foot of the guava tree, as he'd requested.

***

Aparício opens the door to the furnace chamber with a coffee thermos. Ronivon checks the temperature of the retort and notes the data on a piece of paper on the table.

"Good morning, Ronivon."

The man dangles the thermos, smiling.

"I could use a coffee," says Ronivon.

"I made it myself. I hope you like it. I know you're going to miss Palmiro."

"True. I still can't believe it."

"Is today his cremation?"

"Yes, it's today. After the one that's finishing up now. It's going to be hard to toast the old man."

"I can imagine. I've already buried twenty-five of my family and relatives. A whole bunch of friends too. It's really hard. I buried my mother, nine brothers, my dad . . ."

"I know how it is. It's really tough dispatching these folk every day."

"But I don't think I'd be able to cremate anyone. Leave just ashes, dust . . . I don't think so."

"Yeah, Aparício, I thought the same, but I choose to think

I'm erasing all traces. I erase days, years, decades from existence. That's what I'm doing here."

Aparício half smiles and turns toward Geverson, who's pouring himself some coffee. Geverson complains of heartburn and still drinks coffee regularly. The three of them stand looking out the fifty-centimeter ground level window, contemplating the cold, gray day with their hot coffees.

The employee responsible for the refrigerated bodies pushes the door open with a gurney carrying a box with Palmiro's body in it.

"Our old man's here, Ronivon. Fit as a fiddle. Don't forget to return the box," says the man on his way out.

Aparício takes a good look at Palmiro.

"Never had the chance to know him."

"He was a good man," says Geverson, reaching for the thermos.

They stand in silence, finishing their coffee, looking out the window. It's a kind of send-off, since they've stood so often in that same spot chewing the rag.

***

It's been a while since Aparício left, and Geverson took the recently cremated and cooling body into the grinding room. Ronivon opens Palmiro's box. Since the old man didn't have the money for one, they borrowed this box to transfer him from the cooler. He won't be cremated in the box nor will he have an ecumenical service or any such thing. He'll be cremated directly on the tray without a box. Ronivon places Palmiro's body on a marble table and checks his teeth. He's relieved to find the gold teeth are in place. He counts eight again. He opens the door to the grinding room.

"Geverson, have you seen the small pliers?"

Geverson turns off the grinder, which is quite noisy.

"What did you say?"

"Have you seen the small pliers?"

"Here, I have them. Sometimes I need them in the grinder. This thing is a piece of shit. Makes it hard to work. My effort doesn't pay."

Geverson puts his protective eyewear back on and starts pulverizing before Ronivon has had a chance to tell him he'll bring them right back.

Ronivon opens Palmiro's mouth with his fingers and pulls out the gold incisors. These are the easiest to remove, though they require brute force. The hardest are the molars. The molars are all gold. Ronivon gets a hammer and a small knife. He buries the knife beneath one of the molars and hits the handle with the hammer until the tooth is dislodged. Teeth are a challenge to remove; they're deeply rooted, tacked to the bone. When he manages to unstick one, he pulls it out with the pliers. The removal lasts about an hour.

"You really did it, didn't you?" comments Geverson, looking at Palmiro's body upon the marble table.

"He asked, so I had to."

Ronivon's removing the last tooth. This one's really stuck. Geverson asks if he can help.

"No worries . . . I think it's coming," says Ronivon, with a last herculean shove.

His whole body trembles with the effort. The tooth leaps out and Ronivon almost slips backward with the impulse. He places it in a tin cup with the others. He dries the sweat from his forehead; he feels hot and removes his coat.

"There you go, old man. Got them all. You're entire fortune's here."

Ronivon rattles the cup.

"Help me put him on the tray."

"What'll you do with the teeth?"

"Send them to his daughter—wasn't that what he asked? Now I need to find Palmiro's daughter."

Together they put the body on the tray. Together Ronivon and Geverson say a prayer, and each says a few words of farewell before they cremate their friend. Ronivon activates the system that opens the retort door and pushes the tray inside. The flames begin to consume Palmiro. In an hour and a half, only coal will remain.

CHAPTER 7

In Abalurdes bodies continue to be cremated, and contrary to what they feared about raw material being scarce for the crematorium retorts, dozens of indigents and drunks die during the cold early morning hours in surrounding neighborhoods. Temperatures reach extreme low levels. Not even animals resist, like the cows in Mr. Gervásio's pasture. During the day mutts that usually wander the city are collected, all of them dead. Rats that commonly circle the worm farm, keep their distance. Jocasta sleeps inside the house to protect herself from the cold, though she remains in a state of alert. When they open the kitchen door first thing in the morning, she instinctively checks on the worms in the yard. She licks her paws when she finishes her inspection.

Over the past few days Ernesto Wesley has been anxious, and Ronivon has tried seven times to write a letter to Palmiro's daughter. He's been at it since five in the morning, but he just can't do it. Ernesto gets some fresh coffee and makes scrambled eggs on the stove. J.G. sits at the table quietly waiting for his breakfast. Today he'll bury the old man's ashes at the foot of the guava tree by the crematorium garden entrance. Ronivon has found an address for Palmiro's daughter, the same the old man wrote to for eight years without receiving a response.

"Come right out with it, Ronivon. Tell her the old man died and left her an inheritance."

Ronivon scratches his head, rips the last page from the notebook, and sets to writing again without saying anything. Ernesto serves them eggs and coffee and sits down at the table.

"I think you're right. I'll be direct. I'd like to post this today."

Ronivon takes a bite of the scrambled eggs and drinks half a cup of coffee for courage. Well fed, he does feel encouraged.

"Another letter came from him, Ernesto."

Ernesto Wesley doesn't respond.

"I'm going to open it this time," says Ronivon.

"Why?"

"I think he's trying to tell us something."

"Of course he's trying to tell us something, but I don't want to know."

Ernesto eats the rest of the scrambled eggs on his plate and drinks the last drop of coffee. Ronivon hesitates.

"It's bringing me down, Ernesto. I think . . ."

"If you want to talk with him, go ahead."

"But the letters are for you."

"I won't read them."

"Just don't throw them away."

Ernesto Wesley doesn't respond. He puts on his wool hat and a heavy coat.

"Today I've got a forty-eight-hour shift. Will you put out kibble for Jocasta and some sesame seeds from the pantry. Good day, boys, to both of you."

Ronivon says same to you, and takes Vladimilson's letter out of his pocket. He's unable to read his imprisoned brother's letter or to write a note to Palmiro's daughter. He picks up the notebook again and is resolute.

"Dear Marissol,

Your father is dead. He left you an inheritance.

His ashes are inurned at Colina dos Anjos. We need to talk."

He signs his name and leaves an address and telephone number for her to contact him. He folds the paper and puts it in a white envelope. He addresses the envelope but decides to seal it at the post office. He'll leave Vladimilson's letter for later. He pins it to the refrigerator door with a magnet.

***

The line of bodies is long. There'll be fourteen cremations and Ronivon knows he'll have to put in extra hours to finish the job. The first two cremations will be pulverized and the sharp sound of the grinder will ricochet through the room. On his way to work, he stopped at the post office and now is more at ease having mailed the letter. He'd like very much to have news of the old man's daughter, and strangely, Ronivon feels he will soon. Certainly an inheritance should peak her interest. She'll find him and he'll do his part so that Palmiro may rest in peace and that way he'll also feel he's acted honorably among the dead.

Work at the crematorium has been intense. The other retort room has primarily functioned in service of cremating the exhumed, animals, and indigents. It's required hours of service performed by another cremator who comes in three times a week. The intervening days are Ronivon's responsibility. Even when so much is scarce, it's never the dead. Death doesn't have a day off. The more difficult life is the more life generates death. The work it executes is interminable. Ronivon oversees both rooms simultaneously. First he passes the metal detector over the chest cavities of the two bodies. Everything seems in order. He puts them in the retort, and waits for the flames to do their work. In the second room, on the stainless steel tray, exhumed remains of several bodies from a common grave. The parts are mixed, making identification impossible. They're the mortal remains of people who donated their organs to science. Exhumation was necessary to open space for new tombs. He puts on an apron, gloves, and a mask before handling them. He turns the radio to the news, and begins to arrange body parts on a tray that will go into the furnace. Cranium, forearm, hands: the bones are all mixed up. First buried in a common grave, now they'll be cremated on a common tray, ashes will mix forever.

The cremains will be commonly deposited at the back of the crematorium, replete with excrement and trash. After arranging the parts on the tray, he places them in the retort. Then he takes off his gloves and mask. He leaves his apron on.

The heater's been up and running in the crematorium for weeks. The atmosphere's pleasant, however in the basement the effect's not the same as upstairs where it needs to be sufficiently warm for relatives of the deceased to perform ecumenical ceremonies. Central heating keeps hundreds of houses warm in a harsh winter like this.

Ronivon knows very little about what happens up above. From the time he arrives, he's stuck in the basement. He takes his meals—lunch and a snack—in a small room by the stairs. He never goes upstairs. He only has permission to walk on the lower level, and since his delicate work requires vigilance, Ronivon never leaves the incinerated on their own. He communicates with the upper crematorium by way of an interphone installed on his desk, where he now opens the drawer to get Geverson's pliers so he can return them. He hears the grinder pause.

"Geverson, I've brought you the pliers."

"You can leave them over there."

Geverson places the contents from the grinder cup into a labeled urn.

"There . . . 'Dona Brigida' is safely stored," says Geverson. "Look at this here, Ronivon . . . Take a look at these ashes, such fine, uniform grains!"

Ronivon looks inside the urn and admires them.

Geverson pulls off his protective glasses and grabs a new bucket of char labeled "Mario."

"Is that a blender? Looks like," Ronivon is intrigued.

"This is a blender, Ronivon. I can't work only with this old pulverizer. They said they were buying a new one, but until now—nothing."

"Did you bring it from home?"

"Yeah, I did. I think it'll help me do my work faster. It's a very strong blender with many speeds. Take a look, it was a Christmas gift from my mother-in-law."

Ronivon folds his arms and sits in the corner while Geverson works and they talk. It's a peaceful day, cold, like recent days, and he's been waiting for the right moment, and the courage, to open his brother's letter.

He decides to go to the bathroom, and walks to the end of the hallway. The lamp's burned out so he uses the bathroom, as he finds it, in the dark. The retort room door swings open at the push of a gurney with a casket. Another delivery made. A dry echo moves through the hall and ricochets at the back. Sounds produced in the basement resonate to supernatural effect.

Ronivon leaves the bathroom and meets the person responsible for refrigerated bodies in the hallway. They nod to each other in greeting and continue to opposite ends of the hall. Two steps from the retort room door, there's an explosion from inside. He trembles with the shock and feels the vibration from the impact beneath his feet and off the corridor walls. The door swings mightily, and two glass windows that allow you to see inside the room, shatter in a series of bursts.

The main incinerator has exploded and the two incompletely burned bodies are launched in pieces throughout the room; sizzling parts are propelled into the air like small fireworks. The parts in flames scatter throughout the room starting small fire foci on the many papers and flammable objects. Geverson emerges from the grinding room with a fire extinguisher and puts them out. Ronivon calls upstairs and requests help. In a half-hour, firemen are at the scene, including a very worried Ernesto Wesley.

"It was a pacemaker," says Ernesto Wesley.

"But I checked," replies Ronivon.

"Forensics confirmed it."

Ronivon reaches inside the desk for the metal detector and hands it to Ernesto.

Ernesto turns the machine on and tests it over metallic objects around the room and declares that it's defective.

"It was much worse here before you arrived. Geverson and I collected scattered bits of the two bodies. They were all over the room. And all mixed up."

Ronivon's visibly upset. He'll have the rest of the day off just as soon as he's explained to the police what happened, a second time. To the relatives of the dead who are gathered in each of the chapels, they'll say the explosion occurred in an old retort for the exhumed and that they've had to suspend cremations. They're all distraught. The other retort (the old one) next door was unaffected, though the police also require it to cease functioning until the area is cleared and it's deemed safe to return to work. The crematorium supervisor's overwrought.

"Cremation has been suspended until a new inspection is performed that liberates it. The order must be obeyed or there'll be a fine."

These are some of the words the responsible policeman used for his report of the incident. No one was implicated in what happened. Ronivon had previously sent two solicitations to the manager's office requesting repairs or the purchase of a new metal detector. The defective device was taken to the judge as proof, together with solicitations he'd written and sent. Ronivon leaves the retort chamber trailing wisps of smoke, without knowing when things will return to normal.

***

The line of dead bodies doesn't cease to grow. On average five new bodies arrive daily and they're beginning to cramp the cooler. The new retort will take a few weeks to arrive. Bureaucracy demands time and patience. The boss is sleepless, searching for some solution. In three days, the crematorium will receive a visit from investors, and everything needs to flow smoothly. The pile of bodies rising in the cooler is a regrettable vision. But, worse still are the questioning human eyes wishing to know what to do with that pile.

The chief calls a meeting and among those gathered are Ronivon, Geverson, J.G., and Aparício.

"In just three days we'll be visited by investors who want to expand Colina dos Anjos activities, they'll turn this place into the nation's nucleus of death." He straightens his thinning hair and pauses for a moment.

The chief's name is Filomeno. He's a white man with protruding veins on his arms and hands. He wears bottle-bottom glasses that deform his face by augmenting his eyeballs. His hunchback has become more distinct with the years. His hair is falling out. He's got bald spots on his big head. He combs his hair from back to front to hide his baldness. Evidently, this makes his hairdo eccentric, but reveals something of his character. Filomeno's a man who'll cover up any tiny thing that might disturb his reputation, whether signs of aging due to a prominent bald spot, or the company's incompetence in dispatching the dead.

"We have a big problem here, and I know no one wants to lose their job."

The men shake their heads.

"As it happens I want to move this business forward. I'm certain that in short stead we'll be better off than we are now. Much better. And your salaries will probably be reevaluated with a twenty percent increase—what do you say?"

They smile and catch each other's eye. They're excited.

"But before this happens we have to dispatch a room full of bodies, and we can't reject a single one. We're the best in the region—within 600 kilometers, nothing compares to Colina dos Anjos."

The men nod and, between pressed lips, quietly affirm there's no place like Colina dos Anjos.

"I'm going to need your help. Each of you," Filomeno says, a finger raised, and he goes on, "you need to put to rest the eighty-seven bodies that are overfilling my cooler. I don't know what you're going to do, but I know I want it emptied in two days. And your jobs depend on it."

The men look at each other again, without enthusiastic or celebratory murmurs. They're dumbstruck. Filomeno awaits a response. He sits at his desk. He adjusts himself until he finds a comfortable position, and this little ritual is to give the men time to feel encouraged.

Filomeno takes a comb from his pocket and pulls it through his hair from back to front. With open palms he smooths it, finding a place for every hair.

"Men, don't look at me like that. Death doesn't take a break. We need to find something to make this okay. Tomorrow we'll have a big delivery from an accident that happened yesterday. I've heard it's thirty bodies now and climbing. All will be coming here. What'll we do? I won't turn away this merchandise, I've already said I'll accept it."

Ronivon takes a step forward. Cautiously.

"Sir, we don't have anywhere to put so many bodies."

"I know. You have two days to empty the cooler."

"And what'll we do with the bodies?" asks Geverson.

"I prefer not to know," responds Filomeno.

The telephone rings. Filomeno answers, and asks the caller to hold. He tells the men they're free to go, and in two days he'll conduct a new inspection to see if everything's in order. He returns to his call, and the men leave silently, without a compass.

Gathered in a corner of the reflective gardens, shrunken with cold, they discuss what seems to be a tenebrous and inescapable task.

"I think burying the bodies is the only solution," says Aparício.

"I don't know. Digging such a large hole would call a lot of attention."

"We could put them all in a common grave," says Aparício, with finality.

They discuss it for a while, exalting at times, until they find what seems to be the most sensible solution.

"I think we should burn them all," says Ronivon.

"We can't make a bonfire," says one of the men.

"Twenty kilometers from here there's a charcoal works. They have earthen kilns there and they're closed at night."

"Think you could arrange it with them?" asks Aparício.

"We can try. It won't be cheap, but I think we can get the money from Mr. Filomeno."

"And a truck too?" asks Geverson.

"That too. I know the foreman at the charcoal works responsible for the whole place. We play cards on Thursdays," says Ronivon.

"Will we make more charcoal?"

"Yes, J.G., we need to make more charcoal."

Ronivon pulls down the earflaps on his wool cap, and looks up at the sky. The men are pensive. After a few days with the crematorium retorts down, the sky's become less cloudy. Toward the charcoal works, clouds are heavy, like gigantic concrete blocks, and darkened ash is more visible than anywhere else in the region.

CHAPTER 8

The lunar landscape is insufflated with smoking protuberances. Their cocoon shapes are a lot like termite nests or anthills, with a vertical slit similar to the female sex, and all the bulbous structures are pockmarked with valves to allow heat to escape. These rustic clay kilns are aligned side by side over an immense horizontal distance surrounded by still-living vegetation: the little that remains.

The scene is smoggy, smoke trails ride the air up from flues making the charcoal works landscape sinuous and infernal. From a distance high above the valley, his eyes sting from the fog of soot spread by the wind. Ronivon looks out admiringly onto the tiny men walking among the kilns, feeding firewood through the slits, or driving their shovels under the fallen coal, flinging it into a tall, dark pile.

When the soil is contaminated and the rivers are polluted, the city lies sterile. But the inhabitants of Abalurdes draw on the dead nature of char for survival. The ovens are like fertile, birthing women. And life is the char that is also death.

Soot stuffs up eyelids, ears, and throats. These colliers are made blind, deaf, and dumb by the ash. They don't wear gloves, boots, or air filters to breathe, or any adequate clothing. They find it necessary to go about half-naked, skin on display and lungs infected. When they're black and naked they all look alike. They're at the burn ten hours a day, six days a week. Sooty black all over, it won't scrub off because each day they return to the same scene. A spectacle from afar these men appear as shadows.

They become black and undistinguishable by the savage work of transforming living nature into still life to survive.

Some colliers have crushed fingers or lost them altogether with tools used for work. One might have lost a finger, but that doesn't alter their conditions one bit. They're men and specters.

Melônio Macário walks attentively along the alleys formed by the kilns. He checks the operation of each with his experienced eye. His clothes are the color of the sky: charcoal. His gaze is blackened and even his eyelashes are soot-heavy. The taste in his mouth is bitter and the smell of burning coal obliterates all other perfume. Facing a barrel of slurry water, he takes off his straw hat and submerges his head for a few seconds. Despite the cold, the kiln alleys emit intense heat. He raises his head and dries himself with a handkerchief from his pants pocket. He replaces the hat on his head and goes to the makeshift camp.

He approaches a man lying on a dirty and distressed mattress. The environment is grimy with soot. Everywhere eyes burn; breathing's difficult. Melônio Macário touches his arm and whispers the man's name. He's been ill for two days. He's got an intestinal infection and a lot of pain. Today, two other men will take him home.

"Melônio, sir, I'm in pain."

"Take it easy, kid, they're coming get you."

The man motions to a bucket near the bed.

Melônio reaches out and pulls it close. The man raises his head and vomits into the bucket. He's very weak and the pain increases as he's spewing.

"They should be arriving."

Melônio takes the kerchief from his pocket and dries the man's sweaty forehead, soothing him.

"Melônio, sir, I don't want to die here."

"Take it easy, kid, you're not going to die. I'm so old, I've had every kind of illness and I'm still standing. You'll get well."

The man signals for the bucket and vomits again. Melônio's concerned, but doesn't show it. He takes the religious charm that's been around his neck for thirty years and hands it to the sick man.

"Here. Have some faith, kid. You'll get better. Squeeze it hard enough and it'll help you."

Melônio Macário walks outside the workers' camp and calls to a man shoveling coal onto one of the many hideous mountains across the site. The man, with the signal from his foreman, drops his shovel and goes to speak to him.

"Xavier's very sick. Did the men say what time they were coming?"

"No, they didn't, Mr. Melônio."

"But did you call them like I asked?"

"I called, sir. But they didn't say when they'd come."

"I'll send Zé Chico to call again. Tell him to come here and tell Chouriço to take his place."

"Yes, sir."

The man rushes to do what he's been told, and then Zé Chico prepares to go to the phone, six kilometers away, roadside, in front of a gas station.

"Zé Chico, tell them the man's very sick. No one dies while I'm in command. Tell them this. Do you understand? Take my horse and go quickly. I need to get Xavier out of here."

Melônio Macário hands him some coins to buy a calling card at the gas station and tells him to hurry hard.

Before Melônio returns his attention fully to his colliers, Ronivon, who was until then walking around unnoticed, shrouded in smoke, goes to meet him.

"What are you doing here, kid?" Melônio asks surprised, reaching his hand out in greeting.

"Melonio, sir, hello. I've come to talk to you."

"Then say what's on your mind, kid."

"I don't know how to start, but . . ."

"Give me just a minute, I'll be right back."

Melônio goes into one of the alleys and tends to the woodpiles going into the kilns. He yells to one of the men to displace a mountain of coal, from in front of one kiln to the other side of the alley, pointing in the exact direction. The charcoal will eventually be loaded into the back of a truck and taken for packaging at the distributors, some distance from the charcoal works.

Melônio Macário pulls half a cigar out of his pocket and lights it as he saunters back to where Ronivon waits, a bit dazed, in the chaos of the factory. They step a few meters away from the kilns to save Ronivon's eyes from the burn.

"So then, have you figured out where to begin?" asks Melônio.

"Melonio, sir, one of the crematorium retorts exploded and now we're relying solely on the old furnace working. But we've got tons of bodies and the cooler's piled so high they won't fit anymore and the old retort cremates more slowly so it won't account for all them bodies. And it only takes one at a time."

Melônio sucks on his cigar and exhales the aromatic smoke. He mumbles something between thin lips, but Ronivon doesn't notice.

"Tomorrow some investors are coming out, our manager says. Important men who'll invest in the crematorium. My job and everyone else's is at risk unless we find a way to dispose of these bodies, you understand?"

Melônio nods and draws on his cigar again. He's silent for a moment, thoughtful.

"I can free the kilns for you tonight. Come back at six and bring the bodies. How many?"

"Eighty-seven."

Melônio glances at the cigar between his fingers. Switches to the other hand to do some math, mutters something again.

"That's a lot, isn't it?"

"Yes, and they keep coming."

"I have plenty of kilns here, but you'll need to bring all your men. Cause it'll be a long night."

"And how do I pay you back, sir?"

"I'll want a bottle of rum and another of whiskey. But good quality."

Ronivon nods.

"And another thing: I have a very sick man here. Need to get him to a hospital—has to be soon. Did you come by car?"

"On my brother's scooter."

"He's pretty thin. Think you can carry him?"

"I think so."

With the help of another man, they wrap Xavier in a sheet and place him on the bike. They tie Xavier's weakened body to Ronivon's. Xavier hasn't got the strength to hold on to anything, but the religious charm. Ronivon starts the motor.

"Xavier, you need to hang in there, okay? It's the only way. Ronivon, I'll be waiting for you precisely at 6:00."

"Yes, sir, and thanks."

Ronivon returns to the main road as fast as he can on the scooter. It takes twenty-five minutes to reach the nearest hospital. Xavier vomits four times during the journey. Ronivon has an empty stomach and manages not to throw up.

Xavier's treated and medicated. Ronivon leaves him, grateful, in the hospital. He returns home soaked in vomit, reeking and freezing. But things are getting resolved, and by tonight it'll all be over.

***

Ernesto Wesley takes care of the worm farm on his day off. He's surprised that Dona Zema doesn't pester him about Jocasta's persecution of her chickens, and he doesn't hear clacking from her house. It was usual for Dona Zema to spend much of the afternoon out back on the balcony, sewing, kneading dough for bread or cake, or watching the henhouse, where she'd dedicate a lot of time encouraging her chickens to get to work. He thinks she may have been driven off by the cold, or gone to visit a relative on the outskirts of Abalurdes. Ernesto Wesley checks the wire fencing separating his yard from his neighbor's and finds many of Jocasta's hairs. The dog often scratches herself against the barbed wire tips. As soon as he has some available cash, Ernesto intends to make a secure wooden fence. He's already saving up for it.

He spends the day at home without so much as showing his face on the street. In the afternoon, after lunch, he sleeps a little and wakes when someone knocks on the door. He throws a blanket over his head and wraps it around himself when he gets up. He opens the door and sees a young man who works in the neighborhood grocery. It's about a call the grocer received regarding his brother Vladimilson, and the grocer needs to talk to him. Ernesto changes, puts on his wool hat and two coats. Still a few meters from the grocery store, on the sidewalk, he feels apprehensive; his head's erect like an antenna probing the air and his fine hairs bristle. When Ernesto Wesley arrives, he's taken to the back of the greengrocer to a small, crowded space he calls an office.

Ronivon arrives home and goes straight to the bathroom. Takes off all the vomited clothing and leaves it on the back porch. Gets under a hot shower and, ten minutes later, is refreshed. When he comes out of the bathroom, already dressed, he meets Ernesto Wesley at the kitchen table, anguished. Ronivon approaches his brother and touches his shoulder. Ernesto grabs his hand.

"What is it, Ernesto?"

"It's Vladimilson."

"What about him?"

"They tried to kill him."

"Tried?"

"He's in hospital and wants to see us."

"How'd this happen?"

"A fight among inmates, and a guy stabbed him, then set him on fire. They say it's a matter of hours before he dies, and he only talks about wanting to see us."

Ronivon collapses into a chair and holds his head in his hands. They're quiet. Jocasta sticks her head through the open kitchen door and cautiously enters. She lies at Ernesto Wesley's feet and moans. After some time, Ronivon rises.

"I need to resolve a problem at work and will spend the night at Melônio Macário's charcoal works."

"What happened?"

"We need to cremate eighty-seven bodies there. Colina dos Anjos is in trouble."

Ernesto, teary-eyed, seems not to care.

"Pick me up there in the morning. We need to go."

Ernesto nods.

"I think I can borrow the grocer's van," says Ernesto.

"Don't you want to go on the Lambretta?

"I guess we'll need to bring him back with us."

"Sure . . . probably."

Ernesto Wesley and Ronivon say goodbye on the sidewalk. Ernesto heads toward the greengrocer to see about borrowing his Volkswagon Transporter, and Ronivon, carrying a backpack, catches a bus to the crematorium to make good on a long night's preparations.

***

An hour before dark, the men who were able to gather at the crematorium, eight all together, are engaged at the arduous task of piling bodies onto the back of a truck. Filomeno, the manager, borrowed the truck from his brother, a truck driver who owed him some favors.

With an improvised ramp at the back of the truck and the help of two gurneys, they stack the bodies. On the truck bed, J.G., with boundless strength, pulls one on top of the other. Ronivon handles one of the gurneys, and remembers the scene he'd witnessed earlier: firewood loaded into burning kilns to turn to coal hours later. In no time, the bodies are stacked. A crematorium staffer drives, chosen for the job because he was a truck driver before working as preparer of corpses. Three men sit in the truck's cab and another five ride in back with the bodies and a lamp to illuminate them in the darkness.

Twenty kilometers along an inhospitable road, abandoned and unpaved most of its length, they arrive at the location.

Melônio Macário waits alone. His men have gone the two kilometers to the camp, or those who live nearby have returned to their homes.

He's sitting under a lean-to, drinking cachaça, and listening to the news on a transistor radio. He hears the truck arrive, but waits for Ronivon to come to him. He's an old man already, and tired, but he works because it's all he's ever done in life.

Ronivon knocks on the old wood that lines the lean-to, and sticks his head inside.

"Mr. Melônio, good evening, sir. It's all here."

"Did you bring men with you?"

"We are eight, sir."

"Well."

He takes a last sip of cachaça, and overturns the glass next to the bottle on a shelf. The glass has turned yellow from constant use and being unwashed.

Ronivon takes two bottles from his bag and hands them to Melônio, who receives them in the dim lamplight and with a grunt admires their quality. It was exactly what he wanted.

"Let's go now. We have to finish before dawn."

The men, on Melônio Macário's orders, are organized like his day laborers. Used to burning green wood into coal, he explains to the men that the procedure will be the same. The kilns are lit and preheated. Fifteen will be used, that is, they'll be working just one of the many charcoal lanes. Since the place has no electric light, torches line the full length of the lane. The foreman instructs them on how to remove the animal char from the kilns and pile it outside, while another fills a cart with it, and moves it to a location where still others will bag it. Melônio will sell this char to families in the region who use charcoal in their homes for cooking and heating in the harsh cold of winter. Melônio

Macário will mix two types of charcoal, animal and vegetal. Selling it this way, they'll erase all human traces. He barely survives on the money he earns as a foreman, and he sends a part of his salary in alimony to his two small daughters, results of his latest marriage.

The men get to burning. The cold night offers no clues to what dawn will bring. The men have brought coffee and cachaça to warm them while they work, and the intense heat off fifteen kilns will keep them toasty too.

The men remove the first haul of bodies from the truck. Melônio Macário has calculated everything. Eighty-seven bodies cremated in fifteen ovens. Each kiln supports two bodies and that means a rotation of three burns. Cremation will take roughly four hours and that means twelve hours of labor. They'll finish early in the morning, before the dayshift arrives. To increase the heat of the ovens the men feed them firewood and then insert the naked, coffin-less bodies into the blazing kilns.

Melônio supervises and gives orders; the men obey the foreman and complete their functions in silence. While the first batch is cremated, Melônio sits back in his chair and observes. He avails himself of the bottle, pouring cachaça into the yellowish glass, which stays within his reach on a tree stump all night. The bodies smell nothing like toasted wood. The stench is as unbearable as the heavy smoke. It's carnage on the grill. Ronivon warned the men to bring cloths to cover their faces, because he knows the scalded smell of death. The soot that covers the location and the men is funereal, and they avoid touching on the subject. Ash clings to them and they drink to withstand the cold and the sacrilege. The terrible smell spreads throughout the region. It won't have dissipated by morning, and will never be forgotten by these men.

Melônio Macário gives a signal for the first batch to be promptly unloaded and a second batch inserted into the kilns. His control is a bandless wristwatch carried in his coat pocket. Three carts are used at the top of the lane. They shovel the contents of the furnace and, it's true, what remains is only char. While impossible to identify bits of bone as a whole, it's still possible to recognize some parts of the human anatomy. And while some men remove bodies, another group repopulates the ovens with a new pair of corpses. Melônio's concerned about remaining human vestiges and he directs the men to run the truck's tires over the piles of roasted and charred bits to crush it all.

Afterward, it's mixed into a vegetal char pile at the back of the charcoal works. The wheels of the truck crush the remains to dust. Whatever stays on the ground will be scattered by the wind.

The work lasts throughout the night and into the morning. After the first haul is removed from the oven, no one stops to rest. They share in the booze, and are kept warm by the kilns. Nearly twelve hours of work, and when the sun points out the cloudy horizon over another cold day, excessive soot has made them unrecognizable, transformed them into men-shadows. Silence among them and the sound of heavy steps moving from one end of the alley to the other and the swooshing of char from one pile to another is all the noise they make. Ronivon's sitting on the floor with his back against a tree trunk. He observes the men as they finish. It's the final push. As in war, the troops try to disguise the wreckage before they leave. He's very tired and satisfied with how they've managed. The truck's empty; they've left no trace in any corner.

The roar of a Volkswagen van can be heard in the distance. Maneuvering over significant depressions, Ernesto Wesley parks and climbs down. Ronivon remains seated where he is and watches his brother as he looks for him. He greets some of the men, and sees that Ronivon is downcast. He approaches, takes a slow look around, removes his cap, and shakes off the sooty dust.

"Apparently you've had a lot of work to do," says Ernesto Wesley.

Ronivon agrees with a nod.

"Are you all right?"

"I don't know," responds Ronivon.

Ernesto reaches out to his brother and helps him to his feet.

"Don't go there, brother."

"It was sacrilege, Ernesto. I think I'll never forgive myself."

"Ronivon, it takes time, but this too shall pass. You'll see."

"I don't know."

"I've erased all the piles of bodies I've seen over the years as a firefighter from my mind. The smell of toasted flesh, the deformity, the destruction."

"But this is different."

"You do this every day, Ronivon. You're a cremator of bodies. It's what you do."

"I erase the traces," says Ronivon.

Ernesto Wesley embraces his brother and walks over to the men who are finishing the service. They're cleaning up, each soaking a kerchief in slurry water tanks, from which they even drink, and then wipe dirt from arms, faces, and necks.

All, except Ronivon, climb into the truck just minutes before the colliers arrive for their day shift. After saying goodbye to Melônio Macário, Ronivon and Ernesto Wesley get into the Transporter and drive away.

"Don't forget the card game this Thursday. It's not the same without you, kid."

"Sure thing, Mr. Melônio, I'll be there."

Ernesto Wesley, like Ronivon, had a sleepless night. He decided to make corn bread, fresh coffee for two thermoses, and creamed corn. He packed it into a Styrofoam box wrapped in aluminum foil. While Ernesto drives, Ronivon regains his strength by eating and resting a bit. But he can't sleep. Both are apprehensive about the meeting.

"Until we resolve everything, I think we should stick around," says Ronivon.

"I'm not going with you."

Ronivon looks unbelievingly at Ernesto Wesley.

"I have to be at the fire station in two hours. I'm putting you on a bus."

"No, Ernesto. You won't do this to me. He's your brother too."

"You're my only brother, Ronivon. I mulled it over all night—I don't want to see him."

Silence.

"I made coffee, bread, and soup. Take them with you."

"It's not right, Ernesto."

"It has to be this way. I don't care if you're not right with it."

For the rest of the journey to the bus station, they don't exchange a word. And this is how they seem to withstand the weight of the other.

Ronivon descends from the van with his backpack and the food bag Ernesto Wesley prepared, yet not a word. Ernesto yells his name and, with hope in his heart again, he turns.

"Did you turn the compost? Today I must feed the worms."

"Yes. It's ripe. I turned it yesterday."

He turns, downcast, and goes to find the ticket window.

CHAPTER 9

With a shovel back, a man cuts up the clay and spreads it on the ground, while two others sift the clay, making a powdery dirt-heap. Someone puts a huge shovel under the sieved clay and with force loads it into a cart. He takes the cart to a clearing where men are at work, kneeling down before newly made mud bricks. Here twenty men produce the molding. They work squatting the whole time with the whole of the strain thrown upon their arched backs.

Bare hands mold the clay into simple rectangular wooden forms. Two men are responsible for mixing slurry to improve the consistency of the raw material, which also has sand in its composition. They carry a gallon of dirty water, pour it slowly on the small hill, and then turn it over with a shovel.

Everywhere there are armed police officers and trained police dogs. They walk the perimeter and oversee prisoners at work. If not for the police presence, it would be like any other brickworks, but sentenced prisoners from the Abalurdes prison are hired here. Located far from the city center, away from coalfields and charcoal factories, the site is muddy and isolated. The work of making bricks takes place in the prison yard. Inmates are at work eight hours a day with a weekly day off. Other groups tend the garden, the pigsty, and the chicken coop. All receive a salary for their work. For some, being arrested has brought better conditions for their families; with earnings they guarantee the livelihood of those who are far away. There are even those who despair of the day the gates will open and they'll be released.

Freedom for most means not having anything to eat, no shelter, and no work. They fear what's outside those gates.

Not every prisoner can be productive in this way. There's a high security wing for the dogs. Men who barely get along with others. Monsters so cruel and uncouth, their character is their true prison. There's no rehabilitation for that.

On their knees, all in a row, Vladimilson scoops up a fistful of mud and throws it in the mold. He presses the clay into place with his hands, and with outstretched palms smooths the top. He waits a few seconds, and with the help of the handle of a hammer, hits the sides of the mold, and detaches the damp brick. Done, he moves half a step to one side and repeats the process.

After a few hours, the bricks will be stored in a large shed covered in asbestos tile. Production remains in the shed on rainy or cold winter days. On hot days, it's left out in the sun to dry.

There's still no rain, but the promise of precipitation momentarily. Two men carry the molded bricks into the shed, where they're stacked on shelves to dry out for a few days, before going into the kilns.

When rain falls, they continue to work under a protective awning. The protection is more for the bricks than for the convicts.

Vladimilson has a good reputation for not causing problems with other inmates. He's a gregarious and helpful man. For every three days of work, one is reduced from his sentence. The money he makes is deposited into an account. When released, he'll have enough to start life on the outside. Everything's going well, but his brothers' silence weighs heavily on his conscience. He's never had any response from either, but persists in writing. Almost every week he sends a letter.

His crime was accidental, but imprudent. Terribly imprudent. Working with clay to model bricks relieves his guilt. Contact with what he holds to be the origin—man's creation—makes him feel redeemed in the eyes of God.

Months ago one of the inmates provoked Vladimilson. It starts over a soccer match. A disagreement about a penalty call put an end to his days of tranquility. The man stalks him with his eyes, like a foraging dog. He too works in the brickworks together with other men, among them Vladimilson's friend, Erasmo Wagner.

These days are challenging. There's scarcely time to contemplate and various obligations are urgent. In the Abalurdes prison the adopted model has achieved good results. But it's known that the dross of society live there, forever marked by their badness.

While he molds clay, Vladimilson tries to shape his own character with his effort. But he's the exception. Most men are molded in concrete. Some are hard as rock. They're unbreakable in spirit, vile to the bone.

The pottery kilns are cave-like openings carved into a hill, with level shelves to hold bricks where they're baked for hours.

When removed, the bricks are deposited inside a shed, where they're stacked to cool, until they're transported by truck to the distributor.

Erasmo Wagner is warm-blooded even on cold days. He's had pneumonia twice and his lungs are feeble from tuberculosis. He's been disease-free for a year. His body's finally growing accustomed to the extreme temperatures.

It was the end of the day for most convicts, and they began to cluster to be escorted to their cells. Vladimilson was washing his hands in a slurry bucket near one of the kilns. He was alone when he was stabbed in the back. The man didn't say a word, but his distressful breath was accelerated. Vladimilson didn't manage to fall to the ground. He was shoved into the nearest, still-steaming oven—since the ovens are never extinguished. Badly wounded and uttering muffled moans, he can't raise himself out of the fire.

The man joins the clustering group and just one shows up missing in the head-count. Erasmo Wagner had a premonition that day, in the form of heavy black fog overhanging the place.

As if death played havoc there. He looked at the hard-boiled man, intact, showing no indications of his crime. Two police officers start a search for Vladimilson. Others are called for backup. An hour later they find him live roasting in the kiln.

Two days later, Erasmo Wagner takes advantage of an opportunity provided by other inmates, all friends of Vladimilson, to murder the assassin barehanded. He strangles him in his cell. In the morning, the police remove the body without ever again mentioning the subject. The death report attributes cardiac arrest as cause of death. No time wasted on genuine scoundrels. With his ability to throttle necks, they speculate that Erasmo Wagner could remove excess waste from the prison, but he says no. He needs a good reason for it. A personal reason. He's a man of principles.

***

It's early dawn when Ernesto Wesley hears a noise out back. Jocasta, commonly silently alert, is now agitated. He hears the thuds of her euphoric body, scrambling from one end of the yard to the other. He puts on a heavy coat and goes into the backyard with a flashlight. They've got a burned out bulb out back. He calls for his dog, but can't see anything amiss. Still, Jocasta seems strange; she's foaming from the mouth. He crosses the yard, checks the worm farm, the wire fence, the farthest corners, and finds nothing. He speaks quietly to his dog, asking why she's so agitated. He imagines the rats. He calls Jocasta to follow, and goes back to bed. Ernesto Wesley wakes a few hours later with light streaming through his bedroom window. He's forgotten to close the shades. The previous day he was let go early, after just a few hours of work, but now he's on again for a forty-eight-hour shift.

He tries not to imagine Ronivon and what may be happening with him. But can't help it. It's all he thinks about. Puts a pot of water on for coffee. While he waits for the water to boil, takes a quick hot shower. The boiling water he strains through a cloth filter holding the coffee grounds, inserted directly in the mouth of the thermos. It drains and he seals the thermos. Dresses and goes to the bakery near his house; buys bread, sliced bologna, and butter.

He returns home and sits down to breakfast. Turns the radio on to hear the news, and spends about fifteen minutes eating, without haste. He's ready to go to work. His uniform and personal items are in a bag on the living room couch. For him, it'll matter that the day is full. He needs to keep adequately busy.

He finishes breakfast, gets Jocasta's kibble from under the sink and opens the back door.

His dog comes to greet him. He gives her fresh water and puts a generous handful of kibble in each of two bowls, to ensure there's enough food while he's out.

Two dead mice catch his eye near the door. He picks them up and throws them in the trash. He goes back in the kitchen and fetches a packet of sunflower seeds. He puts a handful in a plastic dish for Jocasta, who immediately sits to eat, at peace.

Ernesto finds it strange that Dona Zema's chickens are pecking around his backyard. He looks at the yard next door and all is silent. Deserted. For days he's not seen any movement on the other side of the fence.

Many of the chickens are digging in an open ditch in his backyard.

Strange, because the chickens usually cluster around the worm farm, and none are there now.

Ernesto Wesley approaches the hens intending to frighten them off. He believes they might be pecking at something dead, like a rat, for example. Something Jocasta killed. But, while walking to the hen-occupied site, he thinks, Jocasta would never let chickens peck at her dead rats. She's a possessive bitch, and normally leaves the rewards of her vigil by her masters' door.

Ernesto shoos the hens to reach the center of commotion, where most of them are crowded. They don't retreat, but advance on the hole. Ernesto shoos them forcibly and they flutter to the sides, clucking. Dona Zema's face, hands, and some part of her arm are in tatters. Her bones are exposed. Ernesto wretches. Shocked, he tries to imagine what happened. He looks for Jocasta: eating her sunflower seeds on the porch.

He runs as fast as he can to the public phone at the bakery. He calls his fire station and tells them to contact the police. Without delay, a rescue team arrives at his house and the police follow.

Dona Zema, angered by the attacks on her hens that cross the wire enclosure to peck at Ernesto Wesley's worms, decided to poison Jocasta. She prepared hotdogs with large quantities of rat poison and threw them in the yard for the dog. She lay in wait hoping to watch her eat them, but Jocasta smelled the sausages and abandoned them. Dona Zema took the only steak she had from the fridge, which was thawing for her lunch the next day, and injected it with poison. She jumped the wire fence to convince the dog to eat it. The morning was cold, even Jocasta sought shelter. When the woman came into the yard, the dog went to her and sniffed what was in her hands. Dona Zema dropped steak on the ground and waited. She then felt twinges in her chest and shortness of breath. Her legs felt heavy and she couldn't walk. Dona Zema collapsed with what was perhaps the beginning of stroke, or something like it. With her fallen in the yard, Jocasta spent all morning digging a grave, opening a hole big enough to hold the tiny woman. Dona Zema was still alive when she was buried. The dog then pushed the poisoned sausages and steak to the far corners of the yard. In the morning, Jocasta was very dirty, covered in earth, but all Ernesto Wesley did was to give her a warm bath and caution her to not get dirty again.

The police arrive and permit the firefighters to remove the woman. They find steak and sausages scattered in the corners of the backyard. They take the material to a lab. They discover they've been poisoned, and the medical examiner reports that the woman was buried alive and had turned herself over in an attempt to climb out of the hole she was in. Next day, Ernesto Wesley starts building a wall. This takes all his savings, but with the landlord's goodwill, he'll probably get a few months off his rent.

***

After this whole incident, Ernesto Wesley has to work the night shift. Ronivon hasn't arrived yet, but everything's in order in the yard. There's nothing to indicate what happened that morning. He worries about his brother, and leaves a note asking Ronivon to call him as soon as he gets in. He leaves a phone card for the call, beside the note, on the kitchen table.

There's no call, but no sooner has the sun risen, a sinister accident is reported on the road. A horse is found three-days dead, probably hit by a large vehicle. The road has little movement, which makes a hit-and-run easy. No one saw it happen, but the vicinity population is bothered by a terrible smell. Horse parts are scattered along distant points of the road. Not a single vulture overflies. A curious fact: Abalurdes never sees vultures. The population devours their own dead and remains, turning them to dust. The rotten horse exudes a smell that's worse than anything Ernesto Wesley has ever encountered in his life. It hits him a kilometer away. The closer they approach, the more carrion burns their senses. Protected by masks, gloves and boots, the firefighters spread out to scrape animal parts off the road with a shovel and place them in plastic bags. After they complete this service they're impregnated with the stench. At the station, they bathe, and try to scrub away the smell. The bath also helps Ernesto Wesley shed some heavy memories, since it was on that same stretch of road that his daughter was killed. He usually leaves a rose there. The bath removes the smell of carrion, but the memories linger and he must live with them. He gets sick and vomits under the shower. Even though he's used to seeing terrible things, he's an average sensual man vulnerable to thoughts about his dead daughter.

Finishing his shift, he goes home. Ronivon hasn't yet arrived. He walks to the worm farm and follows his dog's nose to disperse the ant foci. When all is tidy, he sits in the yard, wrapped in a blanket, and falls asleep, Jocasta by his feet.

Wakened by a knock at the gate, he gets up and goes inside. Ronivon walks past him straight to the bedroom with no greeting. He sits on the sofa and waits for his brother to talk to him. After twenty minutes, Ronivon decides to speak. He's visibly tired.

"How'd it go?"

"Went well."

"Well how?"

Ronivon takes a two-liter plastic bottle of disinfectant with a violet label indicating lavender fragrance out of his knapsack. It's half-full with his brother's ashes.

"Say hello to Vladimilson."

Ronivon puts it on the table in front of him and Ernesto looks at the bottle. Ronivon sits in a chair and props his feet on the table. He's more comfortable this way, but no less depressed.

"I resolved everything there. It would've made no difference if you'd come. When I got there, he looked at me, reached out, and went into cardiac arrest. He wanted to say something, but only moaned. The only thing I said was 'fuck!' It was frightening. Nothing else could be said. I ran and called a nurse, but they couldn't revive him."

Ernesto Wesley lifts the bottle of disinfectant off the table and places it in his lap.

"I made arrangements with a small crematorium right there. A cremator friend of mine did me the favor and put Vlad at the front of the line, so I didn't have to wait too long and was able to return today."

"And how was he?"

"Very bad. Vlad looked like a lump of coal. He couldn't have made it. He was destroyed. Faceless. All burnt."

They remain silent.

"Who did this to him?"

"They said it was a fight with another inmate that started over a soccer game."

"He didn't even like soccer much."

"That's what I thought."

"And what'll they do?"

"Nothing. They won't do a thing."

Ernesto Wesley nods his head and stares silently at his own feet.

"Why won't they do anything?"

"I heard another prisoner killed the man who killed Vlad. He was a friend of Vlad's and avenged him. What the killer did to him was totally yellow. He threw Vlad into the brick kilns. Before that, he stabbed him several times. The monster."

"I think we need to write to the inmate who avenged Vlad to thank him."

"I hadn't thought of it. You're right."

"Do you know his name?"

"Erasmo Wagner. He's got little time left to serve out his sentence, they told me."

"I'll write to him."

After saying this, Ernesto Wesley feels bleak. He remains motionless and thoughtful. For a long time he'd refused his brother's letters, but now wants to know more about Vladimilson. Ernesto Wesley lowers his head and cries into the bottle of disinfectant. Ronivon hugs him and the two cry for the rest of the day. It rains heavily the whole time.

That night he began writing a letter to Erasmo Wagner. A long letter. Erasmo Wagner never received letters in prison, and he kept this one in his pocket. When he was released, he visited Ernesto Wesley and Ronivon. They spent some hours talking about Vladimilson and laughing about how clumsy he was. An entire summer afternoon passed like this. At no time did they speak of misfortune, even though they were surrounded by it and terrorized by it. The memories of hurts were suppressed for what was better on offer, and the best thing they had in life was life, and there would come a moment when it would cease for all of them. They celebrated the fact of being alive, even without realizing it. They're men who've learned to carry on and to direct their gaze to the least pitiful point possible.

CHAPTER 10

Many days later, Ronivon takes J.G. home. Jocasta recognizes him as soon as he arrives, but feigns disinterest and focuses on her bowl of sunflower seeds. Ernesto Wesley finishes dehydrating three trays of worms in the brick oven he's recently constructed in the yard. He's received a large order from colleagues at work who are going fishing on their next day off.

J.G. crosses the yard and finds the best place to plant the white rosebush he's brought with him. It's a graft from a rosebush he'd planted in the crematorium's reflective garden. Ernesto Wesley and Jocasta join him. J.G. kneels with difficulty and digs a hole in the Earth. Ronivon pours out Vladimilson's ashes from the disinfectant bottle. He passes the bottle to his brother who finishes emptying it. J.G. messes in the earth and plants the white rosebush. The brothers make the sign of the cross in silence. J.G. looks cautiously at Jocasta who never let him plant anything in the yard during the short time that he lived there. But the bitch remains quietly at rest, observing everything all the while.

"I've finished," says J.G. getting up.

"Now we just wait," says Ronivon

"Soon it'll be spring," says J.G.

Ernesto Wesley says nothing, but puts some wooden slats around the plant to protect it from Jocasta, until the dog gets used to the novelty in the yard. Ronivon gets a rosary that belonged to his mother and hangs it from one of the posts.

Ernesto Wesley feels at peace in concluding this task. Every day he'll look at the rosebush and it'll grow and flower before his eyes. He grabs his bag and goes to work. As he leaves he again makes the sign of the cross, and reads a prayer that's nailed behind the living room door. In his profession, it's not possible to predict what might happen to send him home. But he's used to the unpredictable, to death and its horrors.

***

Colina dos Anjos crematorium is up and running again. No one utters a word about what happened the other night. It's verboten to speak of it. A new coal-maker is received with enthusiasm. When Ronivon crosses through the Colina dos Anjos gates this morning, he perceives a woman standing a few meters away. It's Marissol, Palmiro's daughter. She's young, but tired. Her hair is dyed blonde, and she's wearing tight clothes, and patent leather purple boots. She's smoking and seems agitated.

"Are you Ronivon?"

"Can I help you?"

"I'm Marissol."

Ronivon feels dizzy; he thought the woman would never appear. He thought Marissol might be a fantasy of old man Palmiro's, but there she is. He extends his hand and greets her. He invites the woman to enter the crematorium and wait in reception. Minutes later, Ronivon comes up from the basement.

"He wrote you often during these eight years."

"I received some letters, but I move around a lot. I don't stop in any one place."

"Every day he hoped he'd hear from you."

She remains quiet and lights a cigarette.

"He left you everything of value he had. It's here."

Ronivon hands her a little bag containing the gold teeth.

She checks the contents.

"They're all there. You can count them if you like."

She shakes her head.

"That's a good sum. He had a fortune in his mouth."

She laughs timidly. Nervous.

"He left me his teeth. I never imagined that."

"He only talked of you and said the teeth were yours when he died."

She puts the little bag in her purse, thanks him, and asks where he's buried. Ronivon points to the guava tree and says he's buried there.

"Did you toast him?" the woman asks with a touch of irony.

"Yes, we cremated him."

"That's what I imagined. In this shitty place everything ends up like that. Everything becomes dust."

She's quiet. Ronivon stands before her, waiting for her to smoke a little more.

"It's the saddest place I've seen in my life," she says.

"I've never known anyplace else," responds Ronivon, dismayed.

She finishes her cigarette and throws the stub on the ground. She thanks Ronivon and spins on her patent leather boots. Marissol heads over to the tree where her father's buried. Ronivon nods goodbye and bends down to pick up her cigarette butt. Geverson approaches when he sees the woman has walked away, and the two stand there, side by side, observing her by the tree.

"She's Palmiro's daughter, right?"

"Yes, she came to collect his teeth."

"Nice bait. What did she say?"

"Not much."

Marissol looks at the tree for a while. She speaks and cries a little too. Everything in Marissol amounts to a little. Then she crosses through the Colina dos Anjos gate, and disappears upon turning right.

***

Ernesto Wesley removes corpses from the rubble after putting out the blaze with jets of water. It's been a long day with no break from the cold. Even interspersed rain showers didn't dampen the flames, which—once awakened—consumed without pause. The ashen rain is continuous, and unlike white, delicate snow that whitens everything into a fairy landscape, these ashes do the opposite, turning everything somber and concealing all traces of hope. The fire began in a textile factory about twenty kilometers from Abalurdes center and everything within a full block succumbed to it. Homes, shops, schools, everything, devoured by flames on strong currents of wind. The voluminous black cloud of thick smoke, like a concrete wall, was visible from far off, and mixing with the red flames, created a distorted image in the air that signaled fury, despair, and death.

After controlling the flames, there's the rubble to manage. Rubble caves in all the time and produces more destruction; having escaped the blaze a person is still in danger of being crushed by immense falling structures.

This is a complicated profession. Ernesto Wesley is prepared to leap to his death every day; not to die but to save himself. Palmiro understood that every tooth in his head was a precious asset, and Ernesto Wesley also grasps this: in the end all that remains are teeth. They must be preserved at every sacrifice, so if one day he misjudges and fails to escape the fire he so courageously confronts, he won't become just *carbo animalis*.

Ana Paula Maia was born in 1977 in the Nova Iguaçu suburb of Rio de Janeiro, Brazil. She has published five novels, among them: *Entre rinhas de cachorros e porcos abatidos, Carvão animal*, and *De gados e homens*. Her books have been published in Serbia, Germany, Argentina, France, and Italy, and are forthcoming in the United States and Spain. Her novel, *A guerra dos bastardos* was deemed one of the best foreign police-thrillers published in Germany in 2013. She is also a screenwriter.

Alexandra Joy Forman is the author of *Tall Slim & Erect: Portraits of the American Presidents* (Les Figues Press); and, she has translated Brazilian author Hilda Hilst's first novel *Phloem Flux* (Nightboat Books/A Bolha Editora). She lives in Rio de Janeiro.